THE BEAUTY

REBECCA CONNOLLY

PROLOGUE

*T*he situation was hopeless.

She was hopeless.

Caroline Perkins sat in the dormitory with her friends, her fingers knotting anxiously with each other. It was time for them all to leave Miss Bell's school, and she felt the pressure of the next part of her life more with every passing breath. How was she possibly to be a companion to a great lady of high station? Caroline was barely a passable companion to her friends most of the time, and now she would have to earn her way into Society in this manner?

It was positively hopeless.

"Don't look so forlorn, Caroline!" Adelaide Elliott pleaded as she sat down beside her. "It will make me feel worse, and we need to encourage each other."

"I know," Caroline moaned, rubbing at her brow. "I know. I keep reminding myself that this is a fortunate situation for me, and it is. I just… I think I would much rather trade places with you, Addy."

Johanna Grey released a loud laugh as she tossed herself onto a nearby bed. "Why in the world would you want to trade places? You would rather be a governess like Addy?"

1

"In truth, yes," Caroline insisted firmly. "At least then I won't feel like I am pretending."

"You're not pretending," Penelope Foster reminded her for the hundredth time. "You have money, Caroline, and it is not to be scoffed at. Your uncle saw to that. You may not be an heiress, but you are perfectly respectable, and a companion to a wealthy lady of such a stature as Lady Ashby is bound to give you plenty of opportunity."

Caroline gave her friend a despairing look. "I'm from the London docks. I know it doesn't matter to you all, but it *will* matter very much out in Society. I don't know what my mother and Uncle Paul were thinking when they made this arrangement for me. Taking me directly from the docks and sending me here with girls I couldn't hope to match? And then sending me to Lady Ashby? What is the point? Mama shamed the family when she married my father, there is no reason for any of this to take place."

"I think," Adelaide said slowly, rubbing soothing circles on Caroline's back, "they were thinking that this would be an excellent way to improve and secure your future. I would give anything for that myself."

Now Caroline winced and reached over for her friend's hand. "I'm sorry, Addy, I didn't mean... I know I am fortunate, and I hope you don't think that I..."

"No one thinks you have been snobbish or rude or insensitive or whatever else you think you need to apologize for," Johanna insisted. "Caroline, you really should stop thinking that you are the lowest creature on the earth. Honestly, you may be one of the best."

Caroline gave her a dubious look. "You're biased."

"Bias does not necessarily eliminate truth," Penelope pointed out with a grin. "Caroline, you know you will see something of us in London when we visit. Even Addy will be sure to come with her wards, and I'm quite sure Jo and I will be along. The duke will surely let me, and Jo has her own freedom. Then we will all find proper husbands, even the beautiful governess, and be happy forever after."

Caroline nodded at that, knowing it was what they had all planned on, but the truth of it was that she was not sure how much she would see of anyone or anything. She had never met Lady Ashby, knew nothing about her but their family connections and her address in London.

Until Caroline knew exactly what her situation would be, she couldn't be sure of anything, least of all finding a proper husband.

That, she was afraid, would be a far more imposing task than anything else.

But it was the one task that would save and secure her.

It was the reason for everything.

CHAPTER 1

*A*shby House was a dark sort of place. Not in the sense of containing evil or that it received poor care, but in the manner of arrangement and the style of decor. The tapestries were a deep shade of green, some fading in spots, and there seemed to be quite a few, though the details of each were difficult to make out without candles by which to see them. The wood paneled walls behind them were just as dark, extending up into pale plastered ceilings with rather gothic and shadowed carvings in places.

The dark walls held several equally dark sconces, but only every third held any candles, and each of those only held one. Light from the flames distorted everything, casting long shadows where shadows ought not to be, only adding to the darkness rather than taking from it.

Even the grand stairs were dark, and there was no light to be seen at the top. They must have been covered with rugs or carpet, for they seemed to be nothing more than a cascade of gaping caverns ready to ensnare the ignorant trespasser.

"Oh, really, Caroline Perkins," she hissed to herself as she stood in the currently empty foyer, dripping remnants of rain from her bonnet, ribbons, hair, hem, and cloak onto the floor. She clung to her tatty carpetbag and cast a look at the lone trunk the carriage driver had brought in before abandoning her to the stony-faced butler.

Who had gone to fetch his mistress and had been gone for an age.

Leaving Caroline to the dark, lonely, empty expanse of Ashby House, a place as foreign to her as France, Italy, or Africa.

She pushed a damp and dripping strand of her golden hair off of her brow and behind her ear, exhaling slowly as the urge to fidget raced down her legs.

But she would not.

Miss Bell had taught her better.

So here she would stand. Perfectly still.

And wait.

Above her, she could hear footsteps and the creaking of ancient floorboards. Her heart leapt into her throat and she worked three attempts at a swallow before successfully managing it.

Steady, she reminded herself. *Steady*.

She desperately wished one of her braver friends were here with her, if for no other reason than to make her feel better about the awkwardness of her situation. She was not a shy creature by nature, and neither was she terrified of the world as it stood. On the contrary, she likely understood more than a great many of her classmates from Miss Bell's School for Ladies, given her upbringing and family ties. But time could be a great hindrance to one's former nature, and Caroline was no longer accustomed to being bold or intrepid.

She was a lady now.

She would behave as such.

But oh, it would have been lovely to have Penelope or Johanna by her side. Even Adelaide would have made her feel better, and Adelaide was the most sensible of all of them.

Caroline shook her head slightly and lifted her chin. She would not wish her friends here now, not when she had failed to inform them of the whole truth of her situation.

It wasn't all that bad, considering her fortune was very much intact. But no one with a respectable fortune and handsome enough looks wished to leave finishing school only to become a companion in the hopes of gaining entrance into Society. There was nothing for it, as Caroline had no connections into that world herself, but it was not favorable all the same.

She needed Society if she wanted to have any sort of future or station of safety.

And Lady Ashby had promised Society.

For a price.

Caroline was grateful for it, price and all. She would not have been able to bear leaving Miss Bell's and her friends only to return to her father's house, which had not changed in the last fifteen years, despite their increase in fortune. In fact, her father's house had gotten closer to the docks, and had been placed in an even less ideal location than it had been before.

If she had returned there, she would never leave.

Again, the floors above her creaked, but this time towards the stairs. Caroline fixed her attention there, waiting.

"Oh, if only you were a sturdier girl, Millie Bays. I would be down to see my cousin and already comfortably situated. I fear you may be more unsteady than I!"

Caroline's head tilted of its own accord at the almost chirped tone of voice, a scattered image of Lady Ashby beginning to form in her mind. She had never met the lady and hadn't even known of her existence until she turned fourteen. On that day, she had discovered what plan had been set out for her future, all arranged before her mother had passed. It seemed her mother had managed to salvage some of her family connections, if only just, and only Caroline would benefit from them. It had been beyond imagination, hearing what lay in store. Once she'd got over the shock, it had been the grandest day of her life to be sure, though at this moment she felt far more terrified than enthralled.

The stairs groaned under the weight of their current trespassers, and Caroline lifted her chin in expectation, then lowered it quickly.

Better to appear meek than haughty, even if the action was a play at confidence.

She watched the stairs, step by step, as her hostess gradually came

7

into view, heavily supported by an average sized, but by no means frail, housemaid.

Lady Ashby was not as old as Caroline had expected her to be, but just as feeble. Her hair was a blend of mahogany and silver, her eyes a faded brown, and her skin was a sickly, pallid color. She wore a gown in a shade of mauve edged with lace that was beginning to yellow in places, but all was covered, at least in part, by a thick, brown, woolen shawl that Lady Ashby tried to clutch even as she clung to the maid with one arm and grasped a cane in the other.

In truth, Lady Ashby could not have been much older than Caroline's own father, and that seemed a rather bewildering thought.

"Well," Lady Ashby said without preamble as she reached the main floor and eyed Caroline, "you don't look exactly like your mother, but I won't blame you for that."

Caroline could only blink at the statement.

Belatedly, she curtseyed. "Your ladyship," she murmured.

"Can't hear you, dear," came the barked reply, followed by a rather warm smile. "Part of the curse of being so often sickly. I am old beyond my years, blind beyond my eyes, and deaf beyond my ears. But my mouth works perfectly."

Caroline had to smile and dipped her chin in acknowledgement.

Lady Ashby was before her now and straightened to her full height, which was, in fact, just above Caroline's own, though the older woman seemed so much smaller. She reached out two wrinkled fingers and laid them alongside her jaw, turning her chin one way, then moving her fingers to the other side to turn the other.

"Hmm," Lady Ashby grunted, her eyes narrowing. "Quite a stunning beauty, aren't you, child? In the correct settings, you could be a diamond of the first water. A line of beaux a mile long at least. Does that interest you?"

"No, ma'am," Caroline told her softly.

The older woman met her eyes, which had widened only slightly. "No? Bit of a peculiar gel, are you not?"

"I suppose I must be, Lady Ashby," she replied. "I have never found my appearance to be anything worthy of celebrating. It caused enough trouble with my father's employees before I went to school."

Lady Ashby winced and shook her head. "Best not to go into all that, my dear Caroline. Your mother's choice of husband will have continual repercussions beyond even your lifetime, and we need not dwell on it any further. All settled, and I will help you to surmount those repercussions, if I can. You are in my charge now, and we shall put our combined best foot forward."

Impossibly, Caroline found her throat constricting and her eyes watering at that. It had been so long since she'd had someone with any responsibility over her actually work in her own interest. Her mother had been fiercely protective of her, and even her uncle, her father's brother, had had the good sense to protect Caroline's inheritance, but they were both gone now.

Only Lady Ashby, her mother's cousin, remained.

And her father.

Gratitude unlike Caroline had ever known surged within her and the burning in her eyes intensified. "Lady Ashby, I cannot tell you how thankful I am..."

"Tush!" Lady Ashby put her hand on Caroline's shoulder, applying more force than expected, no doubt using her for balance. "There is no need to thank me, child. This is no condescension on my part. You will be my companion and shall earn pin money for your troubles. And you shall earn every farthing of it. As you can see, I am not an easy charge." The woman gestured to herself, and her wavering frame, with a pointed look.

Caroline could only smile again. "I accept the challenge you claim to present, my lady. With all my heart."

Lady Ashby grinned, and in that grin, Caroline saw a resemblance to her mother that immediately set her at ease.

Ashby House, dark as it was, would be her home, and Lady Ashby would be both her charge and her guide.

All would be well, in one way or another.

Lady Ashby patted her shoulder. "Very good. I will not have you begin your companionship until tomorrow, so for now you must allow Millie to see you to your room and get you bathed and changed. Then you shall return to the dining room for supper with me, and we shall have a little chat. Millie!"

The girl stepped forward and offered her arm to Lady Ashby, who immediately waved her away.

"Not me, you simple girl!" she squawked as she turned and began, unsteadily, to make her way out of the foyer. "Miss Perkins!"

Millie jumped and moved to Caroline, reaching for her sodden cloak and bonnet, her hands almost awkward as they stretched to her. She was quick to divest herself of the garments, giving the maid an apologetic smile as the weight of their dampness made itself known.

The girl's expression did not change in the slightest as she bobbed and turned towards the stairs. "If you'll follow me, miss, we'll see you properly set up."

Caroline eyed her trunk and still clung to her carpetbag. She had seen no sign of a footman, or any male servants but the butler, and there was no possibility of him being able to manage her trunk alone. She supposed she could always come back down for it and drag it up the stairs, if worse came to worst.

It would be difficult, but not impossible.

She darted to the stairs, her eyes casting over to the wobbling figure of Lady Ashby as she continued down the corridor. "Will she be all right?" Caroline asked of Millie as she drew to her. "Lady Ashby, I mean."

"I expect so," Millie replied without much concern. "My lady is very aware of her limitations but tries to push against them. She's not likely to get into trouble. She'll find herself a chair and make herself comfortable until you return."

Caroline wasn't so sure about that, but she could hardly argue in a house in which she was only just barely a guest.

Millie led her to a comfortable bedchamber with an adjoining parlor, both of which were without any sort of airs or finery. Perfectly suitable for a companion, and still within proper tastes for a young woman of society.

She shuddered at the thought. Society. She would never be

perfectly comfortable there, and with her own aims for her future, she had no need to be.

A quiet, comfortable life was all she wanted. One where her finances were secure and her affections in no danger. She wanted to marry for love, if possible, but she would settle for companionship.

Not fortune. Not convenience. Not out of desperation.

Comfort.

But in the meantime, and until then, she would enjoy being a companion to her mother's cousin and let her bestow what patronage she would.

Beggars could not be choosers. Caroline was not quite a beggar, but her options were limited.

Millie turned to her with a welcoming smile. "I hope this will suit you, Miss Perkins. Lady Ashby insisted on having you near her, and the finer rooms are a bit further down."

Caroline shook her head at once. "No, this is perfect. It suits me very well. Anything finer than this and I would be most uncomfortable."

"So would I, miss." Millie looked around with a hint of a sigh, then shook herself and returned to her task. "Right, miss. The footmen will have your trunk up here shortly, and I will see to having a bath brought in for you. Lady Ashby has requested that Sally be your personal maid, if you have no objection."

A maid? She'd never even had a maid at school, and she was supposed to utilize them there. It was the mark of a finished young lady, she had been told.

Well, she was finished, and she needed no maid.

"That's not necessary," Caroline told her kindly. "I can manage without a maid."

Millie's eyes widened. "Oh, no, miss. Lady Ashby wouldn't like that at all. She's especially hired a new maid so that Sally might be available for your use. You must have a maid."

Caroline pressed her tongue against her teeth as she fought against another argument.

It would not be seemly to go against the wishes of her hostess and patroness. And she could not, in good conscience, take away the employment of the new maid because she was too stubborn to allow someone else to dress her hair and person.

Some things she would simply have to accept.

She forced a smile and told her tense frame to be calm, though it refused to listen. "Of course. Very well, then. I would be pleased to have Sally attend me."

If the amount of relief that washed over Millie at her reply was any indication, Caroline would have to adjust to all manner of things living at Ashby House. Imagine having so much emotion over a woman accepting a maid to tend her.

Unfathomable.

"Very good, Miss Perkins," Millie said with another bob.

Oh, this was intolerable. "Caroline, please," she begged.

Millie's complexion paled to match the linens in the room.

"Never mind," Caroline grumbled, shaking her head. "That would be too much, yes?"

"Y-yes, miss."

She sighed and moved to the fire that had been built up, warming her hands. "What are the chances of my being called 'Miss Caroline' instead?"

Millie seemed to think about that. "Give it a few days, miss. We may get there."

Oh, good. Hope at least.

Still, it was better than nothing.

Caroline smiled again, this time genuinely. "Thank you, Millie."

The maid curtseyed. "Mrs. Ramsay will be up shortly, miss, to make your acquaintance and see to your needs."

The footmen appeared then with her trunk, and she could see with her own eyes that there were, in fact, male servants in the house. They set the trunk near the bureau, bowed, and left without a single word.

Caroline took two steps towards the trunk before Millie had a comment.

"Don't do that, miss," she advised, a touch of laughter in her voice. "Leave it for Sally."

Foiled, Caroline turned and sank onto a chair, keeping her posture as proper as could be. "Consider me duly chastened," she joked.

Millie did laugh now and nodded. "You'll get used to it, miss. Welcome to Ashby House." She curtseyed and left the room.

"Thank you," Caroline murmured to the empty space. She glanced around the room, the faint light of evening and candles distorting shadows along the walls. A flash of lightning gave her a moment of illumination, but not in any way that gave her comfort. All of her worldly possessions lay in the carpet bag and trunk beside her, and now she was to be here in this grand house.

She prayed Lady Ashby had no elaborate plans for her, that she might be able to proceed as she wished without interference, and that somehow her father might keep his distance.

He likely already knew she had arrived. He always seemed to know.

Caroline exhaled and opened her carpetbag as various servants began to make preparations for her bath, and retrieved her journal. She moved to the small writing desk in the corner to find a pen, and then, in lieu of a letter, began an entry to her friends.

Dear friends,

You will not believe my journey from Miss Bell's to Ashby House, and the nature of my arrival.

CHAPTER 2

*W*illiam Debenham was a gentleman.

If it was said in the proper tone, the statement would portray all of the derision he currently felt about the words themselves, and likely receive sympathetic nods from those who needed no explanation of them.

He didn't have a problem with being a gentleman. On the contrary, he was well aware that in order to advance in life, he *must* be a gentleman, both by birth and by manner.

The trouble was that Will was *too much* a gentleman.

There was such an affliction, despite any dubious regard for the idea, and he suffered from it.

He had never been so intoxicated as to be unable to walk on his own power. He had never been able to charm a young woman into something within five minutes of making her acquaintance. He had never said anything that would give offense or insult, let alone leave any questioning his better nature.

He had never managed to say no to his mother.

He apologized profusely.

He constantly felt guilt over the slightest perceived misstep.

He was, in effect, a complete milksop.

And, by all accounts, evidence, and observations, milksops did not win on the battlefields of life. Or attain the sort of wives that would make the state of marriage palatable.

Unfortunately, he was at the age where he was expected to view marriage as palatable, and to take action accordingly.

At the present, the only woman in the world that he knew of who had any interest in becoming the next Mrs. Debenham, or, in his particular case, the first, was the sister of his closest friend. And there was nothing in creation or imagination that would persuade him to offer for the hand of Anna Sheffield.

Especially not if his marriage was supposed to be a palatable one.

She was a good enough girl, he supposed, but ardent pursuit of his affections without the ability to sustain them gave the idea of her a rather bitter aftertaste. Will would much rather tolerate his future spouse at any given time than spend an inordinate amount of time avoiding them.

From his experience in Society, only those gentlemen who possessed some level of wickedness in any regard made love matches, and only the fortune hunters acquired heiresses. It was backwards and upside down, and the true gentlemen in the world, especially those without the blatant fortune to attract desperation, were left with the plain, the poor, and the wallflower. If any of the women in those categories had suited him, he would have proposed to them without delay. But as he knew all of them, and had tried to form good opinions of them, and had failed, he was, for the present, still a bachelor.

Much to his mother's horror.

"I don't understand," David Sheffield was saying as they sat idly at their club, his high brow furrowed as he stared at Will. "You wish to be less of a gentleman?"

Will nodded once. "Yes." Then he shook his head. "Well, no. That is to say, yes and no."

The furrows in Sheffield's brow deepened. "Now you've lost me."

"I know," Will admitted with a sigh. "I fear I have lost myself several times on the idea. The thing is, I cannot seem to convince any woman who has in any way raised an interest or curiosity in me that she ought to attempt to raise an interest or curiosity *about* me. My only recourse, as I see it, is to retreat from my perfection and rebel."

Now the dark eyebrows that had lowered over equally dark eyes rose with alacrity. "Perfection? I wasn't aware that had been decreed. Congratulations."

Will chose not to acknowledge the idiocy of his friend and settled for a droll look. "I have been too stringent in my gentlemanly ways and haven't developed any qualities that would make me attractive to the ladies of Society."

"That's not what Anna says," Sheffield mused with the sort of smirk that ought to have rendered him a disloyal brother to his sister. "Especially with you being the son of Lord Sedley. You're quite a catch, according to her, even if you are the second son."

He knew exactly how Will felt about his sister, and he knew what sort of creature she had become. Spoiled, puffed up, condescending, ridiculous... Were Sheffield a bit more of a popinjay, he might have become the same, but he had inherited the better behavior, and thus was resolutely human.

And his loyalty to his sister did not extend to blindness as to her character.

"Well," Sheffield continued when Will did not comment, "how are you going to sin so flagrantly as to render yourself rebellious rather than pious?"

"I'm not pious," Will shot back. "I'm... I'm boring."

"At the moment, yes, I would say so," came the quick retort. "I've never wanted to ignore you more than right now."

Will rolled his eyes, shaking his head. "Now I know that is not true."

"You are lamenting over your good nature and actively considering behaving badly as if it would be an improvement." His friend shrugged without concern. "Besides being an absolutely ridiculous notion, it also seems remarkably high-handed. I have never found you perfect, and I doubt anyone in the world, including my sister, would find you so. You haven't managed a wife because you haven't done much to pursue one. You haven't entered into any courtships because you haven't exactly tried. And you would make the worst possible blackguard in the world, which is why you have not naturally become so. Just accept that you are one of the few genuine gentlemen of the world and embrace the fate."

There was silence for a time as Will considered his friend's words, then he scowled across the table at him. "I believe you said something complimentary in there, but the tone was so full of derision, I'm not sure that was quite clear enough."

Sheffield smiled very thinly. "Good, then I was successful."

It was a trifle awkward to express such sentiments, Will was well aware of that. It made very little sense, and he wouldn't have been able to voice them aloud to very many of his friends if he wished to be taken seriously. He didn't actually intend to commit a crime or tarnish his reputation. He only wished he weren't quite the paragon that he seemed to have turned himself into.

He hadn't even been tempted to cheat at school, and what did that say about him?

"I suspect," Sheffield mused, clearly in the mood to be talkative, "that you might be bored, Deb. The Season is getting underway, and you aren't looking forward to it. Am I right?"

He was right, but Will wasn't sure he wanted to admit that to him.

He made a face and exhaled with a reluctant nod. "You are. I'm not sure I can bear going through the motions again. I don't want to be seen as a man desperately seeking a wife, but I'm also not the sort to engage in the Society, or its social engagements, for my own pleasure. There is nothing to attract me to any of it, and I don't have the excuse of escaping to the country. No one I know well enough is spending time at their country estates at the present, even if I did have an invitation."

"I might be able to help you there," Sheffield murmured slowly.

Will looked at him in surprise. "You don't have your own country estate. And I thought your family were keeping to Hollydale this year."

"They are," Sheffield confirmed. "I'm not inviting you there, and I didn't think you'd want the fuss of the Sheffield children, mob of them that there are."

It was true, Will did not, much as he liked children in general. But he might have accepted any way just for the diversity of his scene and situation. He was never quite sure how many younger siblings Sheffield had, but it was enough to make one's head spin, of that he was positive.

"Then... how are you able to help me?" Will asked, giving his old friend a quizzical look. "Are you inviting me to someone else's country estate?"

"No," Sheffield replied pointedly. Then his mouth curved in a faint smile. "I am inviting you to my aunt's townhouse."

Will stared at his friend for longer than was considered polite, blinking on occasion, waiting for the explanation to come as to how such a thing was supposed to be in any way helpful.

Sheffield was either unobservant, which he knew to be untrue, or he was impudent, which was far more likely, for no such explanation occurred on its own.

"Why?" Will asked, resigning himself to the ridiculous prod.

"Because she loves young people," Sheffield informed him without any hint of lordliness. "She is always wanting guests to come, though not to stay, and she has the perfect ability to say exactly what anyone else would wish without the reservation Society would usually upholds. When she's awake, that is."

None of this was sounding particularly promising.

Will shook his head. "Just how old is your aunt, Sheffield?"

That had his friend laughing. "Not quite aged, thank you very much. She's only graced with a sickly constitution that belies her true age. I quite like her, and I don't say that lightly."

"And coming to call on her would do what?" Will barely avoided making a face as he considered the prospect of calling upon a not-quite-aged, sickly woman of Society simply because he was bored. It certainly wouldn't go very far to helping his too-gentlemanly nature become something more relatable, but it might raise a few questions.

"Help me survive being cooped up in the house with my sister," Sheffield immediately replied.

Will sat up straighter, emphatic shaking of his head beginning without hesitation. "No. No, I'm not coming to stay in the same house as your sister just to spare you the trial. I am not so devoted to your happiness as to sacrifice mine."

Sheffield threw his head back on a laugh. "Heavens, no. Deb, I would never ask you to do that. I do think Anna will behave herself better this time, given this is to be her first Season and she is desperate to make a good impression, but no." He shook his head firmly. "I only need you to call regularly. My aunt requested that I stay at Ashby House, undoubtedly to keep Anna out of trouble, but also as a comfort to her, meaning my aunt. She's really very fond of me."

"Poor lady," Will murmured without much sympathy.

That earned him a cold look, but Sheffield said nothing further.

Could he really spend a dedicated part of his time during the Season calling upon his friend, and, by extension, his friend's aunt, without the visits providing him any sort of true benefit? Especially considering Miss Sheffield would be always about and having her in the vicinity would undoubtedly raise speculation and gossip.

He did not need that swirling around. He wanted to be less of a gentleman, it was true, but not so far gone as to be entirely without sense. He was polite to Miss Sheffield and doubted that would change any time soon no matter what his personal feelings towards her, but anything further than that, even in speculation, would only do him true harm.

"Will others be part of the regularly calling party?" Will carefully queried. "Or be staying with your aunt?"

Sheffield frowned at that. "Well, I doubt we will invite others to stay, as I do not believe Lady Ashby keeps many guest rooms in working order. But I daresay as we engage more and more in the events of the Season, we will surround ourselves with friends at Ashby House. For the present, I really only know you well enough, and we've been friends for years."

It was true, they had been, and that association had been made through their years at school together, not in any real social gathering.

"Your sister may garner some attention for herself," Will pointed out.

Sheffield groaned the self-same sound all elder brothers everywhere must have done when challenged with a younger sister. "I know. One can only hope it will be people with taste and respectability. Lord knows, Anna has never in her life listened to me."

Will nodded, more in commiseration than in agreement. He had not had quite enough experience with Miss Sheffield to say how she behaved with her brother, for good or for ill, but Will did have a sister himself, though Nell was three years his senior. They hadn't listened to each other at any given time in their youth, but their relationship hadn't suffered much for it.

But then, Nell was sweet-tempered, for the most part, and had no airs.

He *had* endured enough experience with Miss Sheffield to say that.

"Very well," he conceded with a heavy sigh. "When you are settled with your aunt at Ashby House, I will call upon you. I will make your aunt's acquaintance, hopefully attain her good opinion, and I will accompany you to select events in Society at my discretion."

Sheffield echoed his heavy sigh, though his was one of relief rather than resignation. "Thank you, Deb. I promise to make this worth your while."

Will managed a smile at that. "I doubt you can actually promise that, Sheffield, unless you are capable of accurately anticipating the unknown."

"I have been known to guess correctly in the past," Sheffield allowed with a sage nod. "That could be our first foray into the path of your sin. Gaming club, perhaps? I do know of one or two, and I won't be free to venture there once I'm ensconced away at Ashby House next week."

There was a promising thought. Will did occasionally opt to venture into the card room when he was forced to attend balls, and his skills at those tables, while not precisely excellent, were good enough to keep him from drastic losses. He never gambled recklessly, and rarely gambled at all, but if he were to make more a habit of cards and gaming…

"Capital idea," he said, rapping a fist on their table and rising. "One can be always at the gaming tables and in the card room and still be a gentleman."

Sheffield gave him a dry look. "Yes, that was my chief concern. How might we best give you faults while still retaining your status." He shook his head and pushed his chair back, rising himself.

"I don't want to be a cad," Will protested as the left the room. "And I have no desire to become a villain."

"What a relief."

Will scowled at his friend's back. "You are being remarkably unsupportive."

Sheffield glanced over his shoulder. "That's because this is idiotic, and I am only indulging you because I know none of this will work."

"It *will* work," Will insisted, already considering his strategy when they sat down to their first games. "I don't think we ought to risk much in the gambling. One does not need to appear without financial responsibility in order to get ahead."

Laughter reached his ears, and his scowl deepened. "You are a terrible sinner, Deb."

"That phrase is usually said with some derision, not amusement," Will pointed out.

Now Sheffield craned his neck to look almost fully at him. "I mean you are terrible at sinning, not that you sin in terrible way. The distinction changes the tone."

Will raised a brow. "Keep that up and you'll find yourself all alone with your sister and your aunt."

Sheffield cleared his throat and straightened. "Right, sensible bets are wise, especially while you try to gauge the other players at the table…"

CHAPTER 3

*W*ithin a week, Caroline had mastered the rhythm of
Ashby House, and was just as comfortable in her new
role as she could have hoped.

It helped that the staff was small, and that Lady Ashby had no
qualms in telling her how she felt, what she wished, and how things
ought to be. Adjustment was really quite simple under those circumstances, and Caroline could adapt accordingly.

She had written to her friends in her journal every day, which
seemed far and away better than writing any of them letters. They
knew of her being sponsored, of course, but she was afraid of admitting her fears to them. How she would almost rather return to the
class of her birth than pretend at the anticipated heights her sponsorship could give her. She could not reveal that, and she would not
burden them with those things. And being as she was, her days were
not filled with any sort of excitement, only the day-to-day busy
activity of a fine house, though without any of the social engagements
that one might have expected.

No one called on Lady Ashby, and Caroline, naturally, had no one
on whom to call. Or to receive, for that matter. And that suited her
just as well.

She would prefer not having anyone call on her presently, or to call on anyone herself.

Much better to live the quiet life she hoped to have in future now while she had responsibilities that were the perfect excuse to avoid going out in society. She needed to make a marriage for herself, that was true, but there was no reason a poor girl from the docks needed such a fuss to find one.

And yet, Lady Ashby had surprised Caroline with tutors almost from the first moment of her arrival at Ashby House.

Tutors. Despite having successfully complete her education at Miss Bell's, she had tutors.

Caroline had made an attempt at protesting the action, but Lady Ashby had insisted that all fine ladies furthered their societal accomplishment education even after finishing with school and governesses. That hardly seemed a thing of truth, but one ought not to make a habit of contradicting one's sponsor, particularly when she was a lady of station.

If she were to be perfectly honest, Caroline was thrilled with the opportunity that training in all the areas of accomplishment would bring her, and that Lady Ashby was giving her such attentions, despite her already generous sponsorship.

Caroline's entire life, up until being sent to Miss Bell's, had been spent at the docks. The house she had grown up in could be seen by any ship entering the London docks from the east. She was, or had been, at one time, more accustomed to the rough behaviors of her neighbors and associates than with anything resembling politeness.

But for Miss Bell's and her friends, she might have been there still, and a girl of her quiet nature would never last long there.

She was determined to take this opportunity to change her fortunes, as it were, or she would never surpass them.

Presently, she had finished her daily instruction in the pianoforte, which was not particularly needed, given it had been one of her few true accomplishments from Miss Bell's. Mr. Timmons came regularly and assisted her in her technique, recommended new music, and his instruction proved to be more of a discussion than anything else.

It was one of her favorite parts of the day.

"Miss Perkins?" Margot, one of the senior housemaids, stood at the door to the music room with a fond smile. "Lady Ashby is asking for you."

Caroline nodded, unsurprised. A week in or not, Lady Ashby had no qualms about calling upon her as though she had been at Ashby House for months rather than days. It had the strangest way of setting Caroline completely at ease in her new role and kept her from being terrified about the future before her.

She followed Margot to Lady Ashby's parlor, which was where her ladyship opted to rest while Caroline was at her lessons. It provided her solitude while keeping her close enough to hear Caroline's music, which she claimed brought her peace. It also happened to allow her to call out her instruction for any other topic upon which Caroline was being educated, should she have felt the need to do so.

There had not been a lesson yet where she had remained entirely silent.

Lady Ashby sat in her usual wingback chair, three cushions visible about her, and her head was laid back, eyes closed. Her lace cap was perfectly placed, as always, though her thick shawl was askew on one side.

Caroline smiled as she curtseyed before the woman, though she wouldn't see it. "My lady."

Lady Ashby's eyes did not so much as flutter, but she did exhale audibly. "Miss Perkins. Today we will receive my dear nephew and niece. They will be coming to stay for the duration of the Season, and I trust that you will behave yourself with the decorum expected of my companion."

Guests? No one had mentioned this to her. The idea of guests joining them gave her pause. It was one thing to be companion to Lady Ashby; it could be quite another to be among her kin.

"I trust I may expect you to welcome them?" Lady Ashby prodded.

"Of course, my lady," Caroline replied dutifully, managing a smile.

Lady Ashby had the ability to sound perfectly haughty and full of condescension while keeping an air of mischief and good humor that seemed a perfect contradiction to the words she spoke. Caroline was not one to cower before intimidation, though she would never call herself bold, so from the beginning, Lady Ashby's quirks had not perturbed her. Finding the light of mischief had brightened everything considerably, and now Caroline found herself amused every time Lady Ashby opted for a stern demeanor.

One of Lady Ashby's eyes opened, no hint of fatigue within it, and she smiled. "I have no doubt of that, Miss Perkins. You are nothing if not perfect in your decorum."

Caroline bit her lip carefully, now fighting a broader smile. "I fear I must contradict you there, my lady…"

"Don't," came the snappish reply. "That is not behavior becoming of my companion." Lady Ashby smiled and opened her other eye, taking in Caroline. "With my niece being about, Miss Perkins, we shall have to have some new gowns made for you. I greatly admire your simple elegance and it suits your great beauty with rather becoming taste, but it will not do for association with Miss Sheffield."

"Association?" Caroline repeated before her good sense could prevent her. "Will that be necessary?"

Lady Ashby raised a brow. "I should say so. Remember, my dear, that you are not only my companion, but in my charge. So, too, will she be. I bear responsibility for the both of you this Season, and though you have differing ideas as to your particular aims within it, I cannot have you appearing unequal in any respect. Association will be inevitable, I fear. You far outstrip her in beauty, as will not be a surprise, but she does have the benefit of great accomplishment. It ought to put you both on a same level when taken on the whole, your birth aside. If I can assist you both, it would be a delight to do so."

Caroline did not like the idea of comparison, and she never had. She knew full well where her position was in life according to station, and her time with her friends at Miss Bell's had rid her of the more disastrous flaws in her upbringing. It hadn't made a difference to many of her classmates, who took no pains to use comparison as a weapon, but to her friends, it had only meant Caroline had a unique perspective on the world.

Since coming to Ashby House, even, Caroline had made strides in her improvement. Her tutors assured her that while she may not be considered truly accomplished, she had accomplishment enough to suit some. Her once harsh accent had become now quite diminished at school, and even more polished, filled with finer manners and airs, when she spoke at all.

Most of the time, Caroline found her thoughts were much better suited to staying in her head than coming out of her mouth, where they became jumbled and practically incoherent with her poor talent for speaking. She was not merely reserved due to her quiet nature, but also out of necessity. She was not intelligent in conversation, nor was she politely ignorant, as all fine young ladies were expected to be. Caroline's opinions, which were many, kept to the vaults of her mind, as she had learned from a rather young age that her opinions were simply unwanted.

Best not to expound upon that with her ladyship.

"Miss Perkins," Lady Ashby said in the kindest voice Caroline had heard from her yet.

Caroline looked at her, bringing her attention back to present, smiling politely.

Lady Ashby dipped her chin ever so slightly. "I can assure you that your situation is not so bad, and some extraordinary and rather favorable matches have been made with far worse. In my mind, there is no reason why you should not benefit from my patronage quite well."

Pleased that her thoughts had been so in line with Lady Ashby's, and that the answer she received was exactly what she would have wished, Caroline nodded without speaking, her throat constricting in an almost painful manner.

"And as for your father being in trade," Lady Ashby went on, fiddling with the edges of her shawl, "I do not mind that at all. I believe it is a sign of a keen mind and financial intelligence, which is a right sight better than most of the gentility can say."

That was surprising in the extreme, and Caroline knew her expression showed it.

Lady Ashby chuckled to herself. "Does that sentiment so shock you? Miss Perkins, I am not so set in the ways of Society that I feel it should be restricted to those of a particular birth. I admire ambition and hard work, though I've never quite had to possess either. Your father has managed to rise from his situation and contribute to your dowry enough to be an excellent candidate in Society, and while your mother certainly sank herself with the connection, it is clear she saw potential where no other could."

Oh, this was unbearable. Much more of this kindness, and Caroline would grow too emotional for being presentable, and she had spent a lifetime avoiding such things. Her emotions were to always stay contained until she had the privacy to do them justice. No other person in the world had seen her emotions get the better of her, saving for Adelaide, Penelope, and Johanna, and even they had only seen it once or twice.

She could not let her patroness see her emotions rise in such a way, and she could not confide in her what this all meant.

And as for the potential in her father... Well, it would be best if Lady Ashby did not know how things truly stood with him. It was undoubtedly true that Caroline's mother had seen potential in him that others had not, but it was not nearly the potential it should have been. Her uncle Paul had been the one to secure her fortune as it was, as much as her father had amassed it.

But her uncle would never have been able to do so had *he* not had a keen mind and intelligence, and her mother's connection with that family had proven effective, though not in the obvious ways.

Family secrets were a tricky business.

Caroline swallowed with difficulty, and only nodded. "Thank you, my lady."

"Such a simple reply," Lady Ashby mused, her lips curving. "No excesses, no demures, no elaboration. You are quite the enigma, Miss Perkins, and I like that very much. Mr. and Miss Sheffield will be here this afternoon. Might I trouble you to read to me before luncheon? You do the thing so well, and your voice alterations for each character are so engaging."

"Of course." Caroline moved to the end table and picked up the novel there, then moved a chair nearby and situated herself there. This had become the routine for them, and the usual activity in which they were engaged. Lady Ashby could not read for long herself, as it pained her eyes, which would then pain her head, but she could listen for an age and enjoy every moment of it.

Books had ever been an escape for Caroline, and she was only too grateful that her mother had taught her to read from a very young age, even while they lived in cramped and poor apartments on the docks. There had always been books at hand, somehow, and because of that, Caroline had never felt shame or despair about the state in which they lived.

She hadn't known any different, of course, but she had been well aware even then that she could only rise so far in life.

That thought had never quite rid itself.

Miss Bell hadn't seen it as a hindrance, and it was clear Lady Ashby did not.

Miss Bell was a romantic, and Lady Ashby was kind.

Time would tell if either of them were correct.

Caroline read for what felt an age, pausing only to make tea when Margot had brought it in, and sipping that tea when her throat began to dry. Every laugh or smile Lady Ashby shared during the reading encouraged Caroline to continue, and when her breathing slowed and deepened, Caroline dipped the volume of her voice in an attempt to lull the woman into her rest.

If their guests were to arrive shortly, it would require a good amount of strength and energy, which Lady Ashby did not have much of. As Caroline understood it, shortly before her arrival, Lady Ashby had suffered a debilitating illness that had rendered her bedridden for weeks, and, having a sickly constitution on her best days, she was struggling in her recovery. Her strength, which had never been good, was slow to return, and her energy was easily depleted.

Being rather inclined to rest and solitude herself, Caroline was ever more convinced that this was the perfect situation for her.

When Lady Ashby had indeed drifted off, Caroline set the book aside and rested her own eyes, letting her body relax from its proper posture and slump into the chair. Even after years of training, the deportment required of a lady of society was not quite natural for her.

The faintest clearing of a throat brought Caroline's attention the door of the room, where Margot again stood, her smile an apologetic one this time. "Begging your pardon, Miss Perkins. There is a letter for you."

Caroline stilled at that. Who knew she was here? And, beyond that, who knew her well enough to write to her after her being here so short a time?

She swallowed and nodded, taking the letter from the tray when Margot approached. "Thank you, Margot."

Only when the girl left did Caroline break the seal, the handwriting within bringing with it a faint feeling of discouragement.

Not from her friends, then. But from her father.

So, it would begin, then.

Chickee-

I hope you have settled in with your fine lady and are making a good connection. Anything to bring the name of Perkins higher.

Have you begun to receive funds for your trouble with the lady? Is it enough to send a bit home for your poor father? I've run a little short of late and would appreciate anything my Chickee girl can send on.

Your father

Caroline shook her head and folded the letter in agitation. She received regular updates from Mr. Hardcastle, her father and uncle's man of business, and the man who saw to her own finances, such as they were. She knew the business was sound, and her father would have no need of her pin money, such as it would be. She was not employed by Lady Ashby in truth and would have no salary as such.

Pin money, yes, as had been agreed upon and as was befitting a young lady in Society, which Caroline was purported to be, for the time.

If her father thought she would spare that sum, meager to the finer station and precious to her, he was vastly mistaken.

He could do nothing good with it, of that she was quite sure.

And why would he have any need of it, if his business was sound?

The bell of the front door rang, and Caroline looked at the clock on the mantle.

It was early in the afternoon, even before luncheon, but hardly premature, if it happened to be Mr. and Miss Sheffield. If it were callers, there would be quite the rush to prepare Lady Ashby for receiving them.

Caroline moved to the door of the room, listening closely. The voices were unclear, but as there were more than one, she could only assume it was their guests.

She quickly went to the window, glancing into the street. They arrived in a simple enough coach, rather like any hack to be found on the street, and their trunks were being unloaded. She could not see the Sheffields themselves, but they were undoubtedly in the foyer by now.

Glancing at Lady Ashby, who was still quite asleep, Caroline slipped from the room to descend below and greet them on behalf of their aunt. Millie was on her way up the stairs and smiled at Caroline as she passed her.

"Would you wake her ladyship, Millie?" Caroline asked in a low voice. "She will wish to greet her guests. I will delay as much as I can with Mrs. Ramsay and see them settled."

"Yes, Miss Perkins," Millie replied as she continued up.

Caroline smoothed her simple gray day dress and moved to the foyer where Margot, Mrs. Ramsay, and Fellows, the butler, were assembling around two fair haired and finely dressed guests.

Terror coiled in her stomach, but she managed to keep her feet moving.

The young woman saw Caroline coming and her eyes widened, her mouth pinching. The young man did not see her, chatting as he was with Fellows, who did not chat very well at all.

Caroline curtseyed perfectly and smiled with all the warmth she bore. "Miss Sheffield, welcome to Ashby House."

"Thank you," came the crimped, too fine tone. Miss Sheffield's bright blue eyes flashed with something Caroline did not understand, and she removed her bonnet and wrap, revealing bright, golden, perfectly pinned curls. She draped her wrap over Caroline's arms and forced the bonnet into her hand. "Mrs. Ramsay, will you show me where I am to stay? And then I desire to see my aunt, of course."

Caroline bit the inside of her lip but kept resolutely still. *Steady,* she told herself. *Steady.*

Mrs. Ramsay's mouth pinched in the selfsame way that Miss Sheffield's had, lines forming from her lips and extending into her cheeks. Her eyes flicked to Caroline, and she exhaled silently, her chin dipping ever so slightly. "Very well, Miss Sheffield," she replied in the coldest tone Caroline had ever heard the warm woman use. "This way, if you will follow me."

Mrs. Ramsay turned and moved up the stairs, the footmen following behind with the trunks.

"Margot," Fellows grunted in his rumbly way. "Do relieve Miss Perkins of Miss Sheffield's belongings. She is not a coat rack."

"Yes, Mr. Fellows," the girl murmured as she sprang forward. She met Caroline's eyes in apology. "I am ever so sorry, Miss Perkins. I ought to have stepped forward to indicate she give them to me, but…"

Caroline waved off the apology and smiled, her cheeks coloring in embarrassment. "No need. Take Miss Sheffield's things to her room," she instructed quietly. "Air them properly. Then you and I will have tea together later."

"Miss Perkins," Fellows boomed with some authority, though very polite, "is my lady's companion, Mr. Sheffield, and her ladyship is quite pleased with her company."

"I am pleased to hear it." Mr. Sheffield bowed to Caroline, prompting a responding curtsey from her. "Miss Perkins."

"Mr. Sheffield," Caroline murmured, taking a few steps in his direction. "I trust your journey was not too tiresome."

The man smiled, revealing fine teeth, his fair eyes full of accompanying good humor. "Not too tiresome, Miss Perkins. I have been in London several weeks, and my sister came by post, much to her dismay. I met her at the coaching station, and we travelled here together."

"Oh." Caroline could have kicked herself for being an idiotic ninny but managed to maintain her smile.

Mr. Sheffield removed his hat and began to turn it in his hands. "Forgive my sister, Miss Perkins," he murmured. "She means well. She has no idea what a companion does or does not do."

"Miss Perkins takes no offense, sir," Fellows assured him, somehow managing to smile at Caroline while answering for her. "She is a very good sort, and we are all well assured that she will benefit greatly from Lady Ashby's sponsorship in Society."

The gentleman looked at the butler in surprise, then back at Caroline with a new regard. "Sponsorship? Indeed, Miss Perkins?"

Caroline lowered her eyes with a nod. "Indeed, sir. Lady Ashby is the cousin of my late mother, and she has seen fit to grant me her patronage after I finished school at Miss Bell's. My father is in trade, you see, and in order that I might make a good match, Lady Ashby insists that I require her influence."

Oh, she had said too much, and would soon venture into rambling. She cast a quick look at Fellows, whose expression was kindness itself. Though the two of them had begun rather stonily, she had come to regard him as another sort of uncle, and one whom she could grow quite fond of.

"My aunt is known for her good taste, Miss Perkins, and her wisdom in her patronage," Mr. Sheffield assured her.

Caroline looked up at him then and was surprised to find warmth and smile there. "She is excessively kind, sir. I am most grateful."

Mr. Sheffield nodded slowly. "And I shall be most grateful, Miss Perkins, if you would think of my sister with the same kindness and consideration as you have just done. She is young, four years my junior, and I fear without your good sense. I think you have a level head behind your obvious beauty, and both will serve you well in Society."

"Thank you, Mr. Sheffield." Caroline curtseyed again. "If you will excuse me, I will see to your aunt. She will be most anxious to greet you."

He bowed, still smiling. "Miss Perkins."

Caroline smiled at Fellows, then turned and moved as quickly as she could up the stairs while still appearing graceful. She felt like such a fool, so tongue-tied and silly. She had never seen a truly handsome man before, and Mr. Sheffield would undoubtedly be considered handsome. He would make a great many ladies happy during the Season, of that she was sure.

And Miss Sheffield was so fine, and accomplished, she had already been told. It was no wonder she had thought Caroline a servant. Caroline had never been with fine people, apart from her friends, who did not act so fine, and she know not how to act still. Despite her training, despite her occasional outings, which were successes, she was still terribly ill at ease.

These were people who would see her daily, quite often at that. She could likely manage the outings and tea gatherings; those were brief moments of pretend. But to be continually examined by people of quality? She could not bear such a thing. Lady Ashby had been intimidating from the start, but now she knew her, it was not so. And she knew Caroline's faults, every single one. Caroline had no illusions of her position here, nor in life itself, but she could not bear to be seen as so low in the world when she was expected now to take part in it.

The bell rang again, and Caroline paused at the landing, glancing down at the new arrival.

A man with dark hair and a fine cut of clothing entered, sweeping his hat off at once. He shook hands with Mr. Sheffield and ran a hand through that dark hair, ruffling it just enough to remove the impression of his hat there.

"Fellows, this is Mr. Debenham," Mr. Sheffield was saying. "He is a great friend of mine, and I have invited him to call upon us at his leisure while we are here. I trust this will be no trouble?"

"Of course not, sir." Fellows took Mr. Debenham's hat. "Welcome to Ashby House, sir."

"Thank you," the low voice replied, the words soft spoken and barely reaching Caroline's ears.

Caroline shifted her weight to continue on, the floor beneath her creaking as she did so.

Mr. Debenham looked up, his eyes landing on her immediately, and she froze as they did so.

He was the handsomest man she had ever seen, though she only had Mr. Sheffield for comparison. Mr. Debenham had perfectly aligned features, more angular than Mr. Sheffield, but with enough smoothness to rival a marble sculpture. The color of his eyes was unclear from this distance, but she thought she saw a hint of green there. And his mouth…

His eyes widened, and she felt something tighten in her chest. Her knees shook, her face flamed, and all she could do was stare at him. Gaping.

Like an idiot.

Caroline swallowed and wrenched herself away, striding carefully towards Lady Ashby's parlor, her cheeks flaming beyond reason now.

He was to call at his leisure, was he? How beneficial, then, that Caroline was to be so very occupied with Lady Ashby's care.

After she was sure that her ladyship was settled and at ease, ready for the company of her guests, Caroline would spend a great deal of time walking about the small garden of Ashby House.

A great deal of time indeed.

CHAPTER 4

*W*hatever angels resided in heaven could not have been so glorious as the creature Will had seen on the landing above him at Ashby House.

Two full days later, and he still could not get her out of his head.

He hadn't stayed at Ashby House long, not realizing that the Sheffields had only just arrived and not wishing to disturb Lady Ashby more than she had already been by their arrival. He hadn't even seen Sheffield since then, and it was quite literally killing him inside to not find him and question him frantically about her.

Perfection in every aspect, she had been, and he hadn't heard her voice, seen her dance, or learned her name.

The depth of her dark eyes, even across the distance between them, had unmanned him, and in the space of time their eyes had been connected, he had forgotten everything he had ever learned in his entire existence, including his own name.

He'd seen a great many beauties in his time, and none of them had affected him like this. He'd thought himself beyond the sensibilities of the fools carried away on whims such as this, but he was full ensnared in this one.

Every rationale had passed his mind in an attempt to rid him of the affliction. Whoever she was, she had been very simply dressed, which could easily mean she was one of the servants.

She could be a heartless, cold, aloof woman without the manners to encourage any sort of connection.

That would absolutely change things for him.

She could be another relation of Sheffield's.

Miss Sheffield would likely have him assassinated for pursuing anyone with whom she was related instead of herself. He could risk that. He was not afraid of her.

There was a dozen more points that Will had concocted, and his rebuttal against each were equally pathetic and determined.

He could only be grateful that he had garnered an invitation to dine at Ashby House this evening and prayed she would be there.

She *had* to be there.

Will was a reserved man, and he had no real powers of speech or persuasion, he knew full well. Perfect gentlemen did not have the same amount of charm as the imperfect ones, and he had yet to manage real sin or flaws to bring him down to a more interesting level.

If the mystery woman were not at supper at Ashby House, he would mercilessly interrogate Sheffield until he knew all.

Heavens above, what if Sheffield were in the same house with her? What if *he* wanted her? He would have complete access to her, to her confidence and her affections. He possessed charm and wit, both of which could easily sway a woman to liking him.

Will's hand formed a fist at his side as he rode to Ashby House now.

Sheffield would pay for such a betrayal, unknowingly done or not.

"Steady, old boy," Will muttered to himself. It would not do to get himself worked up over something that had not happened yet. While that would be the sort of rash action that a less than perfect gentleman, or even a cad might engage in, he rather thought his foray into villainy ought to begin in a less dramatic manner than thrashing his best friend upon his hostess's dining room table.

Surely there were smaller ways in which he might tarnish himself.

If he didn't find his footing with this woman, he would likely find several ways, though perhaps not the ones he would wish to.

Ashby House was soon before him, looking every inch the foreboding London townhouse he had taken it for the other day. There had been nothing cheery within its walls but the angel atop the stairs, and she alone was enough to send him in.

His hat was taken at once upon his entry and he was shown into a sitting room that had a surprising number of people within, most of whom he did not know.

The two he did know grinned in near identical manner.

"Debenham!" Sheffield rose and came over to shake his hand as the others in the room also rose. "Come in, come in. So glad you could come!"

Will looked at his friend wryly. "I wasn't aware there was a party this evening, Sheffield."

"Nor was I," Sheffield murmured to him, his smile forced. "Anna made some friends last night at an event and persuaded my aunt that all were her dear friends now. Lady Ashby is amenable to my sister's desires, no matter how extreme." He rolled his eyes very discreetly.

"Deb!" Miss Sheffield called joyfully, striding over to him in a pale blue muslin that suited her eyes rather well.

He steeled himself, smiled with all due politeness, and bowed in her direction. "Miss Sheffield, delightful to see you again."

She immediately looped her arm through his and tugged him towards the rest. "Come and meet my friends, Deb. You will love them all."

Will seriously doubted that, but he permitted himself to be introduced and paraded about like a pony for her entertainment. His mysterious and glorious angel was not among the gathering, and he felt rather inclined to leave after five minutes, seeing what company he was left with instead.

The ladies were Miss Dawson, Miss Fairchild, and Miss Smythe, all fine and elegant, but simpering and silly, rather like Miss Sheffield herself. Miss Dawson was the most sensible, and the most plain, which he found tended to go hand in hand. She was cousins with one of the gentlemen, a Mr. Gates, who was very intelligent, lively, and quick-witted.

Mr. Rhoades and Mr. Jacobs were cheerful and rambunctious, and quite loud. They seemed to be competing for the attentions of all the ladies, and Will could not tell if it was for sport or in earnest. He doubted even they knew.

Sheffield did not say much among the gathering, therefore Will did not feel he had to either. He engaged when one of them included him in conversation, and did so with his usual politeness, but none of the topics interested him beyond the blandest possible.

Gates tried to bring the conversation to something more inclusive to the entire group, but the ladies and other gentlemen tended towards the trivial.

Will restrained a sigh of despair. Small talk before a meal had never been among his more enjoyable habits, and in company such as this, it was even less so. Even their hostess had not ventured into them, though he understood that she was not a healthy woman, and therefore might not be able to endure the social requirements before supper.

Fortunate lady.

"David," Miss Sheffield suddenly said, interrupting everybody possible. "Where is Lady Ashby? I declare, whatever they have prepared for supper will soon grow cold and inedible."

"Not in my kitchens, I can assure you, my dear niece," a stiff voice replied from the front of the room.

Will turned and felt his heart seize up.

She was there.

Bearing the arm of the woman who had to be her hostess, his golden-haired goddess stood wrapped in a deep plum colored gown, hardly a hint of jewelry or finery adorning her further. She needed nothing else, and beside her ladyship, who bore several swaths of jewels herself, anything else would be outshone with ease.

And nothing should outshine her.

Sheffield rose and moved to his aunt with a warm smile. "Lady Ashby, allow me to introduce our guests to you."

She inclined her head with all the pride and gentility that befitted her, and Will found himself smiling. Lady Ashby was clearly not to be trifled with, sickly manner or not, and he liked that very much.

When Sheffield had introduced them, he faced the room in general. "Everyone, this is Miss Perkins, the companion of my aunt, and a very great asset to her, I am sure."

Miss Perkins looked at Sheffield in surprise, though, Will was pleased to see, no hint of admiration, adoration, or romance. More as he expected she might a wayward brother.

So much the better.

Miss Sheffield rose in a huff, her skirts swishing. "Take Lady Ashby's arm, David, and lead her to dinner. Miss Perkins is a slight creature and our aunt will be in danger on her arm."

Will turned to look at Miss Sheffield in surprise. He knew she was a ridiculous creature, but this was beyond even his expectation. To treat his aunt's companion like this, to disparage her before her face without acknowledging her. And before company?

No one deserved such treatment, servant or not.

Sheffield took his aunt's arm but speared his sister. "I think Miss Perkins has more strength than she appears, Anna. Our aunt is in excellent hands."

Will could have applauded that and would have done had Miss Sheffield not taken his arm again and tugged him behind her aunt and brother. The others followed suit, but there was an unequal number of men to women, so two of the ladies as well as Miss Perkins were left to come without escort.

Miss Sheffield strode past Miss Perkins with a sniff, and Will glanced at the woman in concern, but she seemed completely unperturbed by the behavior.

Had this been customary since their arrival?

The dining room at Ashby House was finely arrayed, but not extensively so. Taste enough for her class without giving offense to any out of it. Yes, indeed, Lady Ashby was a character worth knowing, and a connection worth preserving.

With or without her incandescent companion.

Will situated Miss Sheffield in her seat, as was expected, then moved back to the wall to let the other ladies take their places as well.

"Miss Perkins, do please sit yourself here by me," Lady Ashby declared, patting the seat to her right. "I must insist on having you close. And Sheffield, to my left."

Perfect.

With as much haste as was politely acceptable, Will moved to the seat beside her, situating himself between her and Miss Dawes. It was undoubtedly his best chance for acceptable conversation. And with Sheffield across from them, there was sure to be a buffer as needed.

Supper was served, and conversation began to bubble among the table. Will glanced at Miss Perkins in his periphery and found her to be entirely focused on her meal, only murmuring slightly when Lady Ashby inquired something of her.

It was impossible to tell if this were due to her nature, her station, or the behavior of those around her.

He had to find out.

"How long have you been with Lady Ashby, Miss Perkins?" he inquired after swallowing a bite of potato.

Her eyes flicked towards him, but nothing else moved. "A week, sir."

Her voice held none of the practiced primness he was used to, though he suspected her accent was practiced. Careful words in a natural tone, and something of an earthy nature in the sound.

He liked it at once.

"Ah," he replied with a smile. "And how do you find London?"

A corner of her pert lips curved and something in his abdomen tightened. She turned her face towards him, stealing his breath. "I find it as I have always found it, sir. I am London born and raised."

"Are you, indeed?" he asked with surprise. "And what part of London are you from?"

She hesitated and her face tightened, which made him want to frown. What should she need to fear exposing by such a simple answer?

Miss Sheffield giggled without any hint of warmth. "Miss Perkins is from the shipyards, Deb. Her father is a merchant. Imagine the son of an earl seated beside such a creature! What a laugh!"

Her emphasis on the words were exactly as her behavior had been earlier, with derision and scorn, and Miss Perkins lowered her eyes.

"A tradesman's daughter?" Mr. Rhoades asked with a bit of interest. "Fancy that. How much are you worth, Miss Perkins? Must be a pretty penny to engage Lady Ashby's attention."

"What trade, Miss Perkins?" Mr. Jacobs prodded, joining in with a bit of a teasing note. "Cotton? Silks? I could use a connection in wine, if he does that."

"Oh, stop teasing the poor creature!" Miss Fairchild giggled. "She will melt into the floor!"

"A tradesman's daughter here?" Miss Smythe groaned dramatically. "I pray she has been taught correct manners."

"As far as I can tell," Will snapped, "she is the only one with manners present." He looked around and attempting to effectively silence the rest.

For a moment, it seemed to work.

"For your information," Sheffield murmured kindly, "Miss Perkins' father is the most successful shipmaster in London with a stunning fleet under his care."

"Yes, but can a fortune of fifteen thousand remove the stench of fish and trade?" Miss Sheffield inquired in a carefully mild tone.

Silence reigned over the table.

"Fifteen thousand, eh?" Mr. Jacobs mused aloud. "Not bad."

"Not that it should matter," Will said, still sounding severe despite someone whistling. "Apologize to her."

"It's not necessary," Miss Perkins whispered, shaking her head.

Will gave her a hard look. "It is."

"I should say so," Lady Ashby insisted, rapping the table with her knuckles. "I will not have my companion treated so, and if any present wishes to be so very ill-mannered, they may leave my table forthwith."

Now silence *did* reign across the room.

Lady Ashby grunted once. "As I thought," she murmured as she speared a potato and bit into it for emphasis.

Miss Perkins still looked at her plate, the color in her cheeks heightened to an incredibly attractive degree, had she not been so perfectly mortified.

"They *will* apologize," Will told her in the silence, daring the others to contradict him. "I will see that they do."

Miss Perkins only shook her head. "No, thank you. I would rather forget the matter entirely."

"Good girl, Miss Perkins," Mr. Rhoades praised, looking as though he would clap her on the back as he might one of the men. "Excellent heart. Now, can we commence with our eating? I am famished."

The others began to speak again, murmuring amongst themselves without the noted apology he had hoped for.

Sheffield engaged his aunt in conversation, and Miss Sheffield glared at Miss Perkins with some venom, which did not surprise him.

"I apologize, Miss Perkins," Will said softly, choosing not to look at her as he buttered a roll. "That was entirely uncalled for."

She turned towards him. "Why should you apologize for them, Mr. Debenham? You came to my defense, unnecessary though it was."

"Unnecessary?" he repeated, looking at her fully now. "I would not have done so were it unnecessary. I'll not have anyone malign a person sitting at the same table as I, and I'll tolerate it even less if it is over something as trivial as the occupation of her father."

Miss Perkins' slight brows rose, her dark eyes widening. "Trivial? I think you will find that there are not many individuals who would call such a thing so. Trade is not at all the fashion."

Will smiled at her, feeling quite natural that he do so. "Neither is the simple style of my cravat fashionable, but it does not stop me from wearing it thus."

Her lips quirked, but a smile did not blossom. "I cannot find fault in your cravat."

"And I cannot find fault in the circumstance of your birth," he returned. "Nor from whence your fortune comes."

"I think you must be a rarity among society," she countered, her eyes narrowing in the slightest.

"He is," Sheffield chimed in, keeping his voice down to avoid attracting the attention of those around them.

Will gave him a warning look. "This conversation does not need your input, Sheffield, thank you very much."

Sheffield inclined his head and raised his glass in a very faint toast before sipping carefully.

"How did you come to be Lady Ashby's companion?" Will asked Miss Perkins, grasping whatever he could to keep her talking to him.

Miss Perkins took a cautious bite of chicken and chewed before responding. "She is the cousin of my late mother," she eventually murmured.

"Fortunate for you," he replied before he could stop himself.

That sounded condescending, did it not? After scolding the entire room for bad behavior, he was now engaging in the same.

Perhaps he was well on his way to tarnishing his perfect image after all.

"Indeed," Miss Perkins said without any malice or shame, apparently not taking offense. "She agreed to take charge of me after I completed my education and sponsor me in Society in exchange for my being companion to her."

Now *that* was a surprising arrangement. It would raise Miss Perkins from her current level as a near-servant, though certainly a genteel one, and give her a vast amount of opportunity. With a fortune of fifteen thousand pounds to her name, she would be a very attractive candidate for anyone.

Beyond being so very obviously attractive to the eye.

Companions were not technically servants, really. Companions came from all stations and were respected, as a general rule.

"And are you pleased for the opportunity to go out in society?" he ventured to ask.

"No, not at all," she said at once, making him laugh and drawing Miss Sheffield's critical gaze.

"Truly?"

Miss Perkins nodded once. "Truly, Mr. Debenham. Apart from the opportunity to see my friends from Miss Bell's, I care very little for

Society at all, or going out in it. But I must engage, I suppose, in order to secure my future."

Will wasn't sure he'd ever heard anything more delightful. A woman of her beauty who had as little interest in the workings of the public as he did, and valued social interaction with as much contempt?

He could have proposed now, but he thought that might have been a bit rash and unwise.

He was not that far removed from being a gentleman. Not yet.

"I think you are also a rarity in society, Miss Perkins," Will admitted with a raw earnestness he did not usually reveal.

Miss Perkins looked at him with surprising openness. "I'm not in society, Mr. Debenham."

"Nor am I, to be sure," he told her, smiling with ease. "But you soon will be. And that, you can be sure, will change everything."

"Not if I have anything to say about it," she muttered, her eyes casting over to the glaring Miss Sheffield.

Will sipped his dinner beverage slowly, a satisfied weight settling on his shoulders.

He couldn't have said anything better.

CHAPTER 5

*T*he rain was a comfort to Caroline, and it always had been, which meant she had the comfort often. As a child, she loved nothing more to walk out in it, but now she was no longer permitted to do so. Bearing it from the windows, where it is a poor prospect indeed, was not nearly the same thing, but the sound was comforting.

She could have used some comfort at the present.

Somehow, Caroline seemed to become an embarrassment to Lady Ashby in a very short amount of time, despite her hard work and training, and her previous satisfaction with her. Miss Sheffield had taken great pains to remind her ladyship of certain flaws and failings that Caroline possessed.

She could not say for certain that it was maliciously done, but days upon days of correction was very tedious, and now Lady Ashby fretted about her more than ever. Now looming over Caroline's head was the worry that Lady Ashby's niece could eventually convince her that it was a poor choice to sponsor Caroline in exchange for companionship, and then what would she do?

Everything in the last few days had been geared towards preparing Caroline for the Season in truth, including her being fitted for three new gowns, all for everyday use, as well as some very fine gowns indeed. Caroline thought those quite extravagant, but as she was to be seen in her ladyship's company, it made perfect sense. She could hardly be seen with a simpleton dressed as a common dock girl, though it had been some time since Caroline had been one of those.

These new gowns, however, were somehow both sensible and fine, functional, practical, even comfortable, yet higher quality than Caroline could ever have wished for, and they suited her surprisingly well. The increase in her correction and instruction, however…

"Miss Perkins, do come away from the windows and sit at tea with us."

Caroline turned with a polite smile to Mrs. Mayfield, their hostess for the afternoon, and did as she bid, joining her and her daughter, Kate, as they sat together. Lady Ashby was more comfortably situated across the room with some other fine ladies, and Miss Sheffield mingled with her friends somewhere or other.

They were never without the ladies, it seemed, and they dined with them at Ashby House several times a week. Whenever they would go out, Miss Dawson, Miss Fairchild, and Miss Smythe were present in their company. Miss Dawson was kind enough, and Caroline could see her growing fond enough of the woman if she were permitted to know her at all.

Miss Sheffield seemed determined to prevent any sort of lasting association between her friends and Caroline.

Not that it mattered.

"I understand," Mrs. Mayfield was saying with some kindness, "that you are acquainted with Miss Penelope Foster. We have just recently made her acquaintance and find her to be such a delightful young woman. Kate was so very impressed."

Caroline nodded at the mention of her friend. "Yes, Miss Foster and I were at school together. We became great friends, and she is truly a wonderful person."

"And to be the ward of such a fine duke!" Mrs. Mayfield shook her head in disbelief. "She is well set up, is she not?"

The mention of the duke made Caroline's smile tighten, and she forced her tone not to alter as she replied, "Most well set up."

She would not go into the strain that having such a guardian had caused poor Penelope, and, having not had time to see her friend as yet, she could not know how that relationship had turned out. Or if it had.

"Did she seem well?" Caroline found herself asking. "Did she look well?"

"Have you not happened to see her?" Kate Mayfield inquired, somehow not sounding simpering in the question. "Poor thing, you must miss her dreadfully! She looked well, I think, would not you say so, Mama?"

"I would indeed." Mrs. Mayfield gave a very sage nod at this. Then she smiled and reached out to cover Caroline's hand. "It means so very much, dear, that you would indulge me in coming today. Lady Ashby assured me that you would be a comfortable friend for my Kate here. The two of you are nearly of an age, and being so much in the country, our connections in London are scant at best."

Caroline smiled in return and looked at the dark-haired young woman beside her mother. "It is no trouble. I know very few people myself and being Lady Ashby's companion has given me purpose that puts me far more at ease than the idea of participating in the Season does."

Miss Mayfield shuddered for effect. "Our first ball was such a disaster, Miss Perkins. I could barely get a single word of conversation out, and I only danced twice. I cannot begin to think how I shall go on if that is the beginning."

"I will let you in on a secret," Caroline murmured, leaning close. "I have never danced with a man at all. The dance instructor at Miss Bell's was a woman, and I only ever danced with classmates."

"No!" Miss Mayfield's eyes went round. "But what will you do when you attend your first ball?"

Caroline was about to declare her intention to hide along a wall when another person made themselves known to the group with a flounce of an overtrimmed skirt.

"Miss Perkins," Miss Sheffield snapped, putting one hand on her hip. "Have you seen to my aunt's comfort? Or is she meant to call out when she finds herself in need?"

It was unfathomable that Miss Sheffield should be so bold as to scold Caroline before their hostess about such a thing when the invitation for this tea had been specifically for Caroline, and not herself. But it was not in Caroline's nature to give any sort of retort in defense, nor to remind Miss Sheffield of that detail.

Somehow, Caroline managed a polite smile and turned to Mrs. and Miss Mayfield with an apology. "Will you both excuse me while I see to Lady Ashby?"

"Of course," they replied as one.

Miss Sheffield came to stand beside Caroline's chair, and it was clear she intended to take her place when Caroline rose.

Shy Miss Mayfield would not thank her for that.

"And then, perhaps, Miss Mayfield," Caroline added quickly, "we might take a turn together? I understand you have an excellent orangery."

Miss Mayfield brightened and began to nod when Miss Sheffield tittered. "Oh, no, I cannot see how that would be wise. What if my aunt should need you, Miss Perkins, and you were to be so far away? You are *her* companion, are you not?"

Miss Mayfield looked mortified and Caroline felt her own cheeks heat. "Yes, Miss Sheffield," she murmured. "Perhaps simply a turn about the room, then."

She glanced at Miss Mayfield, who smiled a little and nodded.

Miss Sheffield appeared rather smug as Caroline rose, but then put a hand on Caroline's arm. "I hope you do not think me severe, Miss Perkins. I am only anxious for my aunt, you understand. She is so very dear."

The words were sincere enough, but Caroline had never seen any particular warmth or energy where her aunt is concerned. Truly, Lady Ashby seemed to bore and irritate Miss Sheffield more than anything else.

Left with no alternative, Caroline nodded and went to Lady Ashby, who needed nothing, praised her kindness, and encouraged her confidence with Miss Mayfield. Lady Ashby then proceeded to praise her niece for the thoughtfulness of sending Caroline over, and complimented her dress, hair, talents, and everything else she could to the ladies about her.

Caroline barely manage to avoid rolling her eyes, and excused herself to return to Miss Mayfield, who was only too eager to take that turn about the room with her.

One turn quickly became several, though neither spoke much.

"Gracious, how she watches us so," Miss Mayfield finally murmured, indicating Miss Sheffield delicately.

Caroline glanced over and exhaled very softly at the glower to be found there. "Think nothing of it," she told the girl. "Miss Sheffield does not approve of me. She sees a companion rather as a governess, or a nursemaid. Any social engagement with fine people on my part is met with such looks."

"What would she do if I called upon you?" Miss Mayfield tightened her hold on Caroline's arm. "My mother and I, I mean. Would Lady Ashby permit it?"

"Lady Ashby would," Caroline assured her. "She wishes me to make good connections. The request would have to come from you, I think. With her niece to hand, I would think it only too easy for her to be convinced that I am somehow behaving above my station."

"Oh, dear," Miss Mayfield whimpered. "That sounds a trifle intimidating."

Caroline took pity on the girl and rubbed her arm. "I am sure your mother knows the way of it. Lord knows, I do not."

That made Miss Mayfield laugh, and Caroline smiled at the sound, hoping against hope that here, at last, she might have found a friend in London.

Miss Perkins was not dancing.

To be fair, it was a small party, not a ball, and there were only six or seven couples dancing at all.

But such a vision of beauty should not know the feeling of a chair when any dancing was at hand.

Not that Will was dancing either, but he did not dance.

Did Miss Perkins dance? She must, for were not all young ladies instructed in such things? Did not all young ladies find it to be a most enjoyable entertainment?

Perhaps she did not. Perhaps she was one of the rare few who found little pleasure in it. He would only find her more perfect for it, but if she did happen to love dancing and was only lacking in partners, he would defy all established precepts and dance with her as many times as would be politely acceptable.

If not several times beyond the politely acceptable.

It would make him less of a gentleman, and that would be reason enough to do it.

He'd seen her a few times since that first dinner at Ashby House but hadn't had opportunity for private conversation. Miss Sheffield saw to that, and the rest of the inane Sheffield friends either did not notice her machinations or did not care. They entertained their friends so often, Will wondered if they ever truly left, or if the lot of them stayed over in the guest rooms.

Mr. Gates had a begun to take particular notice of Miss Perkins, which tended to grate on Will's nerves. But his attention seemed rather as one might look at a butterfly through a glass. He discovered, at some occasion that Will had not been present at, that Miss Perkins had some skill with riddles and puzzles. He had begun a challenge with her, and it seemed he had yet to stump her, which gave him great delight.

Will grew more and more proud of Miss Perkins with every puzzle she solved, least of all because she took absolutely no notice of Gates and only seemed mildly irritated by his constant quizzing. He knew that Miss Perkins observed his attention on her, how he watched every exchange, but she gave no indication as to how she felt one way or another. He saw neither approval nor disapproval in her gaze, and ever her expression was composed.

The only hint of distress or consternation he had ever witnessed when her accent, cultivated and practiced as it was, faded and a more natural and easier accent made itself known. Only hints, and never enough to declare her common, but Will, for one, wished to hear Miss Perkins' natural accent, just as it was.

Even if it were the roughest, most common accent in all London, he would love it.

There was nothing common about Miss Perkins.

Nothing at all.

"Deb!"

Will bit back a groan, turning towards the approaching Miss Sheffield, knowing what she would ask. "Miss Sheffield."

"I happen to have a dance free at the moment," she said, completely unabashed.

He raised a brow at her. "I wasn't aware there were dance cards at this gathering. What foresight the Bramers have."

Miss Sheffield tittered a tinny laugh that irked him. "Oh, Deb, how silly you are!"

He was nothing of the sort, and never had been, especially not with her. He returned his attention to Miss Perkins, then wrenched his gaze away to avoid raising any ire on the part of Miss Sheffield. Not that he was so very cognizant of her feelings on the matter, but to prevent any further maliciousness on her part towards Miss Perkins.

"You could ask me to dance, you know, Deb," Miss Sheffield prodded without shame.

"No, I could not," he replied without thinking.

He heard her stiffen beside him. "No?"

He shook his head and glanced down at her with as much politeness as he could muster. "I am already engaged for the next dance, I'm afraid."

Her eyes widened, her mouth gaping just enough to satisfy him. He bowed quickly then strode across the room, skirting the end of the current dancing without issue. He prayed this gamble would pay off, or he would be answering for a great deal more than he would like.

Miss Perkins saw him coming and her eyes widened in the sort of terror he would not have expected from her.

He bowed, smiling without effort. "Miss Perkins, would you care to dance the next with me?"

Her slender throat worked on a swallow. "I fear I am a poor dancer, Mr. Debenham," she murmured, her lips barely moving.

"So am I," he admitted freely. "I'll trod your toes in the first few steps."

A hint of a smile graced her lips. "Perhaps we should spare ourselves. I hardly know which of us would escape less injured."

Will could have outright grinned at her show of spirit and wit, uncomfortable as she clearly was. "But then you would be sitting here still and not partaking in the entertainment at hand. That's not acceptable."

"It ought to be," came her quiet reply, her eyes darting about quickly. "No one else seems bothered."

"If you would not care for dancing," Will murmured, wondering about the discomfort she felt and the distant note he heard in her voice as she spoke of others, "I will not insist upon it. I simply did not wish to see you sitting here alone."

Miss Perkins looked up at him, almost smiling for him, which did unspeakable things to his heart. "You are very kind, Mr. Debenham. In truth, I could not say if I care for it or not. My experience is limited at best."

Was that all? He could remedy that, especially if she would continue to think him kind. "Then perhaps this is the opportunity best capitalized upon, as the gathering is small and informal. Grand events undoubtedly await you, and if dancing is not to your taste, testing the waters here would allow you time to create whatever excuse necessary to prevent it happening again in the future."

He hadn't meant to sound teasing; it was simply not in his nature. He usually envied those that could tease and play with ease, unable to do the same. But with Miss Perkins, he found it less problematic and more a natural thing.

And what was more, she smiled at it.

Glorious creature.

"I think you might be right," came the equally glorious reply.

With bated breath, Will extended a hand to her, and when she took it, his heart evaporated into thin air. Somehow, he led her to the open space with other couples, and her terrified expression matched the horrified one Miss Sheffield wore behind her.

"Miss Perkins," Will murmured when she began to look down the line of ladies uncertainly.

Her dark eyes lifted to his, the edge of panic hovering there.

Will gave her an encouraging smile. "It's a country dance. Watch the lead couple, and the ones following. You'll know the way by the time it is our turn. No one is watching you."

Miss Perkins dipped her chin in a nod, her fingers rubbing against each other by her sides. "Are you so certain of that?"

The words took him by surprise, and he glanced about as surreptitiously as he could.

Blast it, she was right. Several eyes were upon her, despite the small number of guests. He should have gathered as much. She was an exceptional beauty, and, dressed as she was in a fine but simple gown of cream and gold, her natural beauty was on display. She would attract attention wherever she went, high standing or low, and at a grander event than this, when she was even more elegantly arrayed...

He would not get within five yards of her then.

Now it was he who seemed to have the difficulty swallowing. "Ignore them all," he managed as the music struck up. "Follow my lead. I'll keep you safe."

Something he said apparently amused her, for she gave him a true smile, small and delicate as it was. "That was never in question, sir."

He would find himself on bended knee before her by the night's end if she kept this up, and he still knew no more of her character and nature than what a handful of moments could allow.

He didn't care. It seemed enough for now.

Marriages were entered into for far less.

But perhaps Miss Perkins had her own mind for her future, including that of marriage and family. She was a unique woman and he could hardly expect her to think of suitors in the same way that a woman like Miss Sheffield would.

What *did* Miss Perkins want? How did one go about discovering such things without appearing forward or crass?

A less gentlemanly man would have come out and asked. Would have found a clever way to work a flirtation and suggestion into conversation, making the object of his affections blush prettily and offer an honest if daring reply to satisfy his curiosity.

Will hadn't managed to become such a man as yet. He would not know the way to do the thing any more than he would know how to lead her in a waltz worthy of her.

He was still a perfect gentleman, for his limited sins, and perfect gentlemen did not inquire about such things.

So, he would stew in his anxiety and feel the queries crawl within his chest until they would expel themselves in a perfectly horrid manner at the most inopportune time, which would prompt his excessive apologizing, and even a creature as patient and kind as Miss Perkins would find him tiresome.

He would not win her then.

But for now, he could fight those questions, and, for the moment, he could dance with her.

He watched her as she watched the other dancers, smiling to himself as he observed how her mind worked on the blessed planes of her face, a crease of diminutive nature creating a faint shadow on her fair brow.

A quick mind she had, that much he already knew, but he could see now the intensity of it as well.

Would her body follow the pattern of her thoughts with as much skill and efficiency?

The motions of the dance rippled their way down to them, and from the very moment she moved, Will felt himself soaring a bit above the company.

Her body followed better than her mind, grace and elegance exuding from even her smallest finger, and the smile she wore, uncertain as it was, captured everything he had seen in her within it.

Dancing was a grand entertainment, Will thought as he took her hand and led her to follow the other couples down the line.

A grand entertainment, indeed.

CHAPTER 6

*Y*our father is struggling financially, Miss Perkins, and there is *no polite way of saying so. Between his drinking, gambling, and the poor market of late, he may not be able to keep all of his ships. We've already had to cut down the fleet, you remember, and to reduce it even more would lessen profits in the future, most likely, but we cannot afford to keep the ships we have now, nor to pay the crew adequately. Since the death of your uncle, your father has invested unwisely with men at gambling tables, so there have been significant losses to the savings of the business. Be assured that your fortune is safe, not being tied to the business at all, and it actually nearer to twenty-five thousand pounds now. I would strongly suggest that you make some more permanent and very strong alliances very soon, as things are likely to only get worse.*

I shall write again when I have news.

Your humble servant,

James T. Coolidge

Caroline stared at the letter in horror. The news of her fortune being greater than previously estimated gave her no pleasure at all, considering the rest of the contents.

She had been receiving regular notes from her father requesting funds, and she had responded to each just as she had the first. She had no funds to spare, and a polite reminder that she did not earn a regular salary, as she was not a true employee. She would only receive pin money, and none of that had come into her hand as yet. She had not added that she would turn none of it over to her father, as it would have raised his ire, which could only create more trouble.

What could she possibly do with this? Mr. Coolidge was very kind to keep her informed, but she had no stake in the business itself. Her father would never have trusted a woman, no matter how capable, to have a hand in any of that. She could only presume that he was well aware of the requests she was receiving, and of the danger her father's declining behavior could bring about.

She rubbed at her brow, sighing in irritation and folding the letter again. There was nothing she could do from here. She would not breathe a word of this to Lady Ashby, and would do her best to remove her own emotions from it as well. During Lady Ashby's prolonged rest tomorrow, she would take a hack down to the docks. Her father would be at the warehouses during the day, so she would be able to move about freely without his interference. Their old land-lady, Mrs. Briggs, would undoubtedly know the truth of matters. She had always liked Caroline, and she would not protect her from the ugliness of the situation.

It was a reckless idea, travelling down to the docks unaccompanied and being unchaperoned about London, but she was a dockyard girl. Dangers in the city had been her childhood companions, while finery was a stranger still. A short visit would do no harm, and she had no enemies to fear.

"Miss Perkins."

Caroline turned, slipping the letter into the pocket of her morning dress. "Yes, Millie?"

The upstairs maid curtseyed quickly, giving her an apologetic smile. "Miss Sheffield and her friends request that you join them in the drawing room."

Caroline raised a brow, making Millie laugh. Miss Sheffield had recently ceased her torment of Caroline, for torment it was, but only because Caroline was suddenly useful to her. The ladies were invited to a house party hosted by some woman of consequence, for which they would depart on the morrow. Caroline was not to attend, which relieved her, and it was expected that the women invited were to participate in riddles or cleverness.

Miss Sheffield was not at all clever and had no wit. Thus, Caroline was a convenient asset.

"I presume they are practicing riddles once more," Caroline murmured.

"I cannot say, miss," Millie replied. "I was not present prior to her request for you. But that kind Mr. Debenham has just joined the party, so it might not be all bad."

Caroline could only nod to that and proceed as she was bid. Lady Ashby was lying in this morning with a headache, but she would ring for Caroline if she was needed. There was nothing to do except indulge Miss Sheffield, lest she spread rumors or cause trouble before her departure.

The drawing room was filled with all the usual friends, though Caroline thought the hour still too early for many callers. Such things didn't seem to affect this particular group, aside from perhaps Mr. Debenham, but he was there too, though without the same jovial air as the rest.

He was always somehow apart from the rest, even when he was among them.

Caroline averted her eyes from his compelling gaze and focused instead on those that had sent for her.

"My dear Miss Perkins!" Miss Sheffield said, sounding far too polite as she came forward to take Caroline's hands. "You are just the person I need!"

It was a feat indeed that Caroline kept her expression blank. "Oh?"

"Indeed!" Miss Sheffield nodded excessively. "I require your assistance. This party at Lady Lawson's estate is to be filled with cleverness and riddles. You are so adept at them; I simply must beg you to assist me in preparing for the event."

"Pardon me, Miss Sheffield," Caroline responded with all due deference, "but I thought it was not seemly for a woman to be clever. I believe you told me as much only last week."

Mr. Debenham, who was still all politeness and reserve, stifled a laugh at that, and Caroline barely managed to keep her attention from drifting to him.

Miss Sheffield only smiled. "You are so bright, Miss Perkins. Too bright and too clever, and you remember so well. Yes, my dear, that is true. But in this case, it is a gathering of clever, witty creatures, and so one must participate and put forth a good show, or else embarrass the rest. You would not wish me to embarrass myself for all to see, would you?"

Truth be told, Caroline would like that very much, but she could hardly say so.

"Very well," Caroline demurred with a dip of her chin. "If you will permit me, I will write down some riddles for you, and you may work at them. Then we might be able to discuss them and see if there are any tricks with determining an answer."

Miss Sheffield's eyes lit up. "Yes! Oh, you clever thing, tricks to getting the answers would be the perfect thing." She gestured to the writing desk nearby. "You will find paper at your disposal there. Is there any riddle you might give me now? While you prepare the rest?"

Did she expect Caroline to create a riddle out of thin air? Miss Sheffield was as ignorant and slow as any woman Caroline had ever met, and likely more so. Anything she attempted before company without practicing would have to be of the simplest kind, and if her friends had even a little wit, they would find Miss Sheffield entirely without it.

Caroline's mind raced, and she seized upon one riddle she recalled from childhood that a ship captain had given her once. "The more there is," she recited carefully, "the less you see. What is it?"

Creases appeared in Miss Sheffield's typically clear brow, and her mouth tightened. "Very good," she quipped without enthusiasm. "I shall think it over." She turned back to her friends to confer, leaving Caroline's path to the writing desk unencumbered.

Caroline moved there and took a sheet of paper, thinking for a moment before beginning to compose the next riddle she could recall.

"Rhoades," Mr. Jacobs suddenly said from his relaxed position on his chair. "Do you think we might have a chance of getting Miss Perkins to laugh today?"

"Oh, I don't know, Jacobs," Mr. Rhoades drawled in his usual languid way. "She does not do so on normal circumstances, and I do not believe either of us are particularly amusing."

That was a true statement, and Caroline ignored their teasing. They had attempted such other teasings before, and Caroline never rose to it.

It only encouraged them, she found, but there was nothing to be done about that.

"She is a reserved creature, is she not?" Mr. Rhoades went on. "I wonder if she is capable of laughter."

"Surely she is," Mr. Jacobs scoffed. "All women laugh, you know. It is part of their nature. I'd venture Miss Perkins' laugh is only more musical than one might think, and thus she is saving us all from being swept away on its melody."

"Come, Miss Perkins," Mr. Rhoades prodded once more. "Tell us true."

"I can assure you, gentlemen," Caroline said with some clarity as she continued to write, "I can laugh, little though I do so. It is quite the same as anyone else's laugh, only softer."

"Oh ho!" Mr. Rhoades chortled. "Such a sound does exist! We must draw it out of her, Jacobs, indeed we must. Sheffield, have you heard her laugh?"

Caroline took no notice of what Mr. Sheffield replied, or any of the others. She only focused all the more on her task at hand. The sooner it was completed, the sooner she could vanish from their midst.

"Miss Perkins, I beg you not to laugh for them."

Caroline glanced up in surprise to find Mr. Debenham standing rather close, though his attention was fixed on the others in the room, his back to the wall. She glanced over her shoulder at the rest, still discussing her and teasing without her notice.

"Please," Mr. Debenham said in a low voice. "Do not laugh."

She gave him an odd look and said, "I have no intention of doing so. I am not being coy, Mr. Debenham. It is true that I rarely laugh."

His bright eyes slid to hers. "They think you are playing a game," he said, almost scolding.

"I never play games," Caroline replied calmly with a shake of her head. "I have no taste or talent for such things. Truth be told, Mr. Debenham, I am the plainest, most boring girl that ever attempted to breach Society's boundaries. And that is no false modesty, that is pure and simple truth." She glanced over at the other men again, who were now attempting to listen in.

Caroline cleared her throat and returned her attention to her riddles. "And there is nothing anyone ought to wish to hear in my laugh," she told him in a much lower tone. "They would be sorely disappointed by it, if it should happen."

"I think there could not be a more precious sound in the world than your laugh," he murmured, his voice very soft.

Her breath caught at the earnest note in his voice, and she raised her eyes to him once more.

His gaze was fixed on her, intensity radiating from his very being. "Not least because it is so infrequently heard. I only beg you not to share it with them because they would not know to treasure it. And you deserve nothing less."

Several heartbeats passed before Caroline remembered that one ought to breathe on occasion, and even more passed before she recollected that she ought not to stare at a man so blatantly. But he was staring back, and there was no course but to return the favor.

In doing so, Caroline found the opportunity to study the man as she never had yet, and what a study he made. Mr. Debenham had a bit of a rough look about him, though without the accompanying grime she had learned to expect from it. For all his finery, he was broad of chest and chiseled of features. He could have very easily pass as a worker of the docks, if he dressed as such. His eyes, so vibrant in their shade, were never hard, but so full of life and light, a captivating energy that the rest of him never seemed to portray.

She found herself suddenly fascinated with his mouth, of all things. The lips were of a moderate fullness, nothing to give one pause, but there was a careful edge to them that made Caroline think that he used to smile a great deal. He was so restrained in public settings, even among their company. He seemed on the verge of smiling often, yet his jaw could be so set that one wondered if he ever smiled in his life.

He had smiled for her, she recalled, and always with gentleness. Never broadly, even when in good humor, but certainly enough to touch her heart.

His manner of speaking was not as rich as the rest, his accent a bit harsher even to her ears. Perhaps that was what made her so much more comfortable around him. And his voice had a touch of the brogue to it rather than the more delicate and cultured Society tones. If he were not bound to London by family ties, or to the general area by heritage, what would entice him to engage in the Season at all? Reserved as he was, kind as he was, gentlemanly as he was, what drew him hence?

He was a puzzle, to be sure, and a complicated one at that.

Caroline was not sure she could figure him out, even with her skills and wit.

But oh, how she wished she could!

MISS SHEFFIELD WAS EVEN MORE stupid than Will had thought her, and that was saying a great deal. Even Sheffield was looking aghast as he considered her, and he had been raised under the same roof.

Every one of the riddles that Miss Perkins had laid out for her had been met with poor answers after extended effort and debate, and an excessive amount of fluster that was completely unnecessary. Each of the riddles were simple and uncomplicated, yet Miss Sheffield had never even come close to correct in her answer.

Poor Miss Perkins did her very best to offer up tips and advice, but there was nothing to be done.

The part the ladies were to attend would be a nail in the coffin of Miss Sheffield's portrayal as a woman of cleverness, from which there would be no recovery.

Even her friends were beginning to look concerned about the prospect.

And now the inane concept of secretly sending an express rider to fetch answers from Miss Perkins in London had been suggested and was now being debated by the company present. It seemed the house was not so far out of London, so Miss Perkins could manage such easily, though it was unclear how Miss Sheffield would afford to pay the servants to ride back and forth. And how such a deal of time could be spent between riddles without the attempts becoming obvious.

It would never work, and several of them knew it well, though none were taking pains to say so.

Miss Perkins merely sat among the company, unable to escape, and mutely accepting whatever decision was made.

Excellent creature, though far too docile at the present. She was no servant in this house, and yet she was content to be treated as one.

He could not bear it.

Yet he was too much the gentleman to rage against it or to demand it be otherwise.

He was trapped between his politeness and his desire, and the way through was clouded by the fog that had come from her very first riddle. Which, consequently, had been the answer to it, as he had ascertained very quickly.

Miss Sheffield had not ascertained it at all and debated endlessly when it was revealed as such.

Will would give anything at the present for the weather to have been fine enough to escape the house for a time, then return when he had clarity. And when Miss Perkins might have been freer to converse with him.

His chest tightened at the thought.

"Oh, I've had enough of puzzles and riddles," Rhoades groaned, suddenly pushing away from the table and rising. He craned his neck and began to pace, chuckling to himself. "I'm not even attending this gathering, and my mind is cramping at the thought of one more blasted riddle. Let us find something truly entertaining to do."

Miss Fairchild giggled and eyed Rhoades with interest. "What sort of entertainment do you have in mind, Mr. Rhoades, hmm? Shall we have some music and dancing?"

Rhoades looked at her as though she were mad. "I said entertainment, Miss Fairchild, not torment." He eyed the individuals in the room in speculation and, as Will suspected, his attention stopped on Miss Perkins.

So did everyone else's.

"Ah ha," Rhoades murmured.

"What?" Jacobs demanded, looking between Rhoades and Miss Perkins. "What are you thinking?"

"I am thinking," Rhoades said loudly, "about the sort of man Miss Perkins might be seeking in London."

The ladies in the room gasped with all the dramatics Rhoades could have hoped for, while the rest of the men looked speculative, if amused.

Will, for one, could only blink.

He generally did not care for Rhoades, and he would never wish to pry into Mis Perkins' private thoughts.

This particular topic, however, he was perishing for insight on.

His gentlemanly nature would allow the lapse in judgment. For now.

Miss Perkins, however, had frozen, and the faintest hint of disbelief was evident in her face.

"After all," Rhoades continued, "I do believe it is our duty as her friends to assist in finding him, whoever he might be. And surely that is Lady Ashby's assignment for the Season."

"I would hardly call it an assignment," Miss Sheffield protested hotly, her cheeks coloring in bright splotches. "Miss Perkins is the one who is a *companion*, after all."

Will bit the inside of his lip in lieu of scowling openly. There was no need for her to throw around the position as though it were no better than the upstairs maid. A companion was a respectable position, and there was some debate as to whether it was a position at all. Some earned wages as employees would, others were family members who were almost shadows for their charges.

A companion was nothing to sneer at.

Mr. Rhoades apparently had a similar opinion. "And what would you call a sponsor for the Season, Miss Sheffield? What other purpose could your aunt have for bringing Miss Perkins out at all?" He turned back to Miss Perkins, folding his arms and eying her with interest. "It is a husband hunt, I bet my best weskit on it."

Will took the chance to look at Miss Perkins, who returned the gaze of the room without any hint of embarrassment or shame. She did not even appear to hold a degree of tension in her face or frame.

She could have been the world's most beautiful, composed statue for all her reaction.

And she said nothing.

"What sort of man should he be, Miss Perkins?" Jacobs inquired, propping his foot on the chair beside him as he surveyed her. "I'd wager would could snag you an earl with your looks."

"Ooh!" Miss Smythe squealed with a clap of her hands. "Yes! Let us get her a man with a title! Oh, what a fine lady of the *ton* Miss Perkins could be!"

Miss Sheffield harrumphed at the thought and grumbled under her breath.

"Such lavish parties, too," Miss Fairchild added. "If we snag the right man of title and fortune, she could be the most enviable hostess of them all." She smiled with a devious air. "I shall require invitation to every fine soiree, Miss Perkins, for my share of getting you a husband."

"Surely not too fine," Mr. Gates commented, surprising Will by chiming in at all. "Miss Perkins has a more reserved nature, that must be taken into consideration. She may not wish to host such festivities, enjoyable though they might be for the rest of us."

Yes. It was high time that someone noticed that simply because

Miss Perkins possessed the glories of heaven in her looks did not mean she wished for the attention of a diamond of the first water. It was plain for all to see that she was not as concerned about social engagement as the others, so why should the idea of hosting events at some grand estate tempt her at all?

"We could still get her a title," Miss Dawson suggested with kindness, offering Miss Perkins a friendly smile. "There is nothing like a title for security and respect, and who would not wish for that?"

Also true, and the thought irritated Will for no good reason. His father had a title, after all, and his brother would inherit one. It didn't make them saintlier, but it did render them quite popular.

Rhoades scoffed loudly. "Because no one with a title has ever done anything to risk his family name, heritage, fortune, or property. It's money Miss Perkins needs to marry for security, and only money is secure."

So there was a bright spot, then. Money could be got. Titles were a bit more limited.

But she *had* money, had she not?

"But what of her dowry?" Miss Fairchild said with the first sign of intelligence. "That is money, right enough."

"Not enough to hide her birth, not nearly enough."

A rapid discussion on titles and fortune bounced around the room between the lot while Miss Perkins sat quietly in her place. Was anyone actually going to inquire of the woman in question what her thoughts were on the subject of a husband?

Will could not ask her. He *could* not. He had far too much interest in the answer, and there was no polite way to bring the topic back to her thoughts.

Why did he care about politeness in this? It was time to stake a claim, to offer himself as a prospect, to declare his horse part of the race that seemed to so amuse the others.

Yet here he stood, silent, staring, and steaming.

"Why not ask Miss Perkins, then?" Sheffield asked, bringing the discussion in the room to an abrupt end, and earning himself unending gratitude from Will that would never go expressed.

All eyes were on him for a moment, then slowly turned to Miss Perkins, who looked horror struck for the first time.

"Well, Miss Perkins?" Miss Sheffield almost sneered. "To what sort of man do you aspire?"

Miss Perkins swallowed once, her fingers knitting with each other until her knuckles turned white. "I have never given it a particular amount of thought," she murmured with surprising caution.

"Oh, come, come," Rhoades protested. "You must have done. All ladies do."

What would Rhoades know on the subject? Will speared him with a look briefly, though it was not seen.

"Let her speak, Rhoades," Gates scolded, keeping his attention on Miss Perkins. "Go on, then. Give it some thought now."

Yes, Will pleaded in his mind. *Please give it some thought.*

Miss Perkins wet her delicate lips quickly, color beginning to rise in her cheeks. "I suppose... I would think a simple country curate would do very well for me."

A ripple of shock cascade through the group, and Will, for one, found his attention somehow more fixated on her than ever.

"Interesting response," Sheffield mused, speaking for them all. "Why?"

"It would be a comfortable living," she said quietly, suddenly lowering her eyes as her voice wavered. "Very safe, quiet, and without much to trouble or distress any. A man of the cloth must abide by rules and boundaries, be an honest man, and think of others before himself. All of these things I desire, and I believe I could make a very good wife for such a man."

Was a more perfect answer given by any woman who ever lived?

Will was tempted to drop to his knees, pray for forgiveness, and take himself off to join the clergy at that moment, but wisdom restrained him. He glanced about the room, and saw that, while the men looked impressed, the women were not at all.

"Oh, Miss Perkins," Miss Fairchild giggled, "we can do far better than some stiff, stodgy clergyman!"

"Indeed we can!" Miss Smythe declared.

"I should hope so." Miss Sheffield sniffed and left no doubt that she was not referring to Miss Perkins with her words.

Will couldn't look away from Miss Perkins, not even in her obvious discomfort. How could she grow lovelier with every additional minute he spent in her company? With every glimpse into her mind, he found her more a picture of perfection than met the eye.

And what met the eye was beyond description in itself.

"If you will excuse me," Miss Perkins murmured to no one in particular as she rose from her chair, "I will see to Lady Ashby now." She bobbed a curtsey and moved towards the door, passing directly in front of Will as she did so.

His fingers brushed against hers somehow, and he thought, or perhaps imagined, that she stuttered a step at the exact time his lungs seized on a breath.

Fanciful thoughts indeed as he watched her go, lingering even as she vanished from sight.

Tempting, but all-too fanciful.

CHAPTER 7

*T*he docks had always smelled the same. Sea water, fish, sewage, and a hint of smoke, all wrapped up with the occasional gust of sawdust and wood on the air.

It had been years since Caroline had been down here, but the scent of home was one she would never forget.

Home. What a peculiar notion.

She'd never quite felt at home anywhere, but when her mother was alive, there had been nothing better than their house on the docks. Mrs. Briggs would give Caroline a fresh biscuit every time she and her mother delivered the rent for the month, as well as the occasional sweet. Errands to the local shopkeepers and vendors followed, though it occurred to Caroline now to wonder about the legality of the wares sold by some of the vendors.

It had not been an idyllic childhood for her, but it certainly could have been worse.

Far, far worse.

Looking at the sort of place it was now, how dark, dank, and filthy everything was, Caroline appreciated all the more that her mother and uncle had had the foresight to send her away to school when they had. Caroline had been blessed to resemble her mother in looks, and in all the favorable ways, and a woman with such looks could find herself in the worst of situations in certain corners here.

She couldn't remain long now, or she might suffer the same.

Drawing the hood of her cloak more tightly around her, Caroline trod the somehow still familiar path to the boarding house where Mrs. Briggs presumably resided.

A series of short whistles rent the air, and, out of sheer habit, Caroline kept her eyes straight ahead.

The whistles came again, this time more in a sing-song tone. "Lovely," a man slurred from somewhere nearby. "Come 'ere, lovely. Papa's 'ad a long day."

"Oy!" another called. "Give 'ee a fiver to set me t' rights!"

Caroline's cheeks grew more heated with every step, wishing it was darker out or later in the day, but it would have been far worse if she had come later. Midday was one of the only safe times. Such comments were not pleasant, or tasteful, but they were harmless by comparison.

"Let me make 'ee soar, lovey," an older man offered. "Give 'ee wings I will."

She turned down a street, away from the callers and the sounds of creaking ships in port and pressed a chilled and gloved hand to her now flaming cheeks.

What would have become of her had she not been sent away from this place? A shiver coursed through her entire frame at the thought.

If her friends could see her now, they would have been aghast. They'd have scurried her away from this place and found another way. Or they would have linked their arms through hers and marched with her to the boarding house.

One or the other.

If not both.

"Steady, Caro," she muttered, surprising herself with her raw, natural accent, which hadn't been used in several years.

She had a sound purpose in this venture, and she would not be swayed.

The boarding house loomed before her, somehow smaller and

dirtier than any of her memories led her to believe. The windows, however, were exactly the same. She was convinced the streaks of dirt, the cracks, and the suspicious stains were all just as they had been in her youth, even if the filth on the building itself had increased.

Why she should notice such a thing was beyond her.

Exhaling slowly, Caroline entered the boarding house itself, stepping into the small but tidy foyer and looking around for anything familiar.

She saw nothing.

The decoration had changed, the arrangement had changed, even the rugs on the floor had changed, and there was not a soul about. Perhaps she had been mistaken and Mrs. Briggs had moved on. This place could have been run by anybody, and possibly someone with no connection to Caroline's father, or her past.

There would be no help for her if that were the case.

A tarnished hand bell sat on a desk nearby, and Caroline moved to it, lowering the hood of her cloak. She rang the bell just once, and its tinkling sound seemed to reverberate off of every surface.

"Coming!" a female voice bellowed from somewhere distant.

Caroline racked her mind for memories of Mrs. Briggs in an attempt to match the voice.

She had no such memory.

A few guests entered the foyer and shuffled past Caroline without greeting her, jostling her roughly and forcing her back until she almost sat upon the desk itself. She was certainly not in the more societal part of London now. No manners or deference, and no gentlemen to see to her comfort or safety. She was no lady here, only a woman, and, if she was not careful, she would be identified as one of finery.

She wasn't anything fine in truth, but the quality of her gown alone would set her apart.

"Oye! Treat a woman with some dignity, will you?" screeched the same female voice from before, making Caroline grin without shame, which was a rarity for her.

Mrs. Briggs was indeed here, but it took her roaring in indignation to jar the recognition for Caroline.

Then the woman herself was before her. Hair a little whiter than in years before, but the overall appearance of the pudgy woman remained the same. The wings of lines from the corners of her lips were, perhaps, a little deeper, but perfectly familiar.

And it was clear from Mrs. Briggs' expression that Caroline had changed enough over the years to be beyond recognition.

"Can I help 'ee, madam?" Mrs. Briggs asked as she wiped her hands on her stained apron. "We're a mite full at the moment, but I can make some of the rest budge up for 'ee."

"Mrs. Briggs," Caroline greeted with a smile. "My name is Caroline Perkins."

The wide eyes of the woman went wider as she scanned Caroline up and down. "Bless my soul, o' course you are! Spit of your mother, an' so! Come 'ere, you blessed angel!" She enveloped Caroline in a warm hug, taking no thought for any differences in station, in fortune, or anything else. Which was just how Caroline wanted it.

She hugged the older woman back and let her kiss both cheeks repeatedly.

"Look at 'ee!" Mrs. Briggs squealed, pulling back and pinching one of Caroline's cheeks. "Beauty beyond compare, Angel, just as I always vowed. Not quite so tall as your mum, but a perfect height all the same. Can I fix 'ee a cuppa?"

"I'd love one," Caroline replied on a sigh. "And... I need to ask about my father."

"Aye," Mrs. Briggs said with a knowing nod and a wave. "Aye, I'd have told 'ee even if 'ee 'adn't asked. Come along, we'll settle it all, an' so." She gestured again and led the way down to the kitchens.

Caroline followed, though she'd have known the way without help. While the foyer and parlor were all changed, the structure of the rooms themselves had not altered in the slightest.

Strange the things one noticed.

Soon enough, she was seated at the same wooden table at which she had sat as a girl, sipping a cup of tea and feeling more herself than she had in quite some time. And, strangely enough, though Mrs. Briggs in no way resembled her mother, she felt more at home.

"Ah, Angel," Mrs. Briggs sighed after a particularly long drink of her own tea, into which she had added a hint of something from a flask in her apron pocket, "I can't tell 'ee anything worthy about your father. 'Ee know 'e's been renting 'is 'ouse from me."

Caroline nodded, fiddling absently with her teacup. "Yes, I remember."

Mrs. Briggs only shook her head slowly. "Twice late on 'is rent at the 'ouse now, even though I've reduced it to just the one room and parlor. 'E always smells of strong drink, and 'as been too often at Mrs. Bradshaw's door."

That stunned Caroline and she could barely swallow, even when taking another sip of tea. Her father had never been one for loose women before, but to be so bold as to go to the very establishment that supplied all of the dockyards with their women? She hardly knew her father, it seemed.

"And his business?" Caroline murmured after eventually managing to swallow.

"I can say nothing o' that," Mrs. Briggs replied as she adjusted her position on her rickety bench. "Never comes up in conversation. 'E don't tell, and I don't ask. But I can't think it's going well, Angel. Not well at all."

Caroline nodded very slowly, the motion more of a ritual response than a genuine one. The revelations required some answer, and she gave one, though she could not have said what it meant.

She could have gathered as much about her father from the state of his letters and what Mr. Coolidge had said but hearing the truth of it made the reality all too certain.

"A pity, Angel," Mrs. Briggs bemoaned. "Such a pity."

Caroline glanced up at the plump woman. "What's a pity?"

Mrs. Briggs' mouth formed a puckered line. "That your uncle was the one to meet 'is Maker afore 'twas proper. 'E'd've set 'ee up right, mark my words. 'Ee take more after 'im than your father, in looks and in temper. Same twinkle in the eye, same smirk when 'ee think. People did talk when 'ee were a babe, but no one ever said aught."

They said... *what?*

Caroline had never heard so much as a whisper of such a thing in her entire life, and *now* it would come to light? Of course, it was only rumor and gossip, and only here where she had been raised, so there was no true risk of it finding its way into Society, or to Lady Ashby. But Caroline didn't fit perfectly there, and she did not fit perfectly there. And an illegitimate child did not fit anywhere when making a good match was the end goal, even it was only in rumor.

Could it be true?

Surely she would have been told. Surely someone would have known or said. She had always favored her mother over her father, so how was anyone to suspect anything?

She wouldn't believe it. Couldn't.

Rumor and suspicion only, and all that in the past.

Caroline nodded to herself, forcing a small smile. "Yes, I do miss Uncle Paul immensely. He would have kept Father from much trouble. He was the one to provide for me in a way I'm not sure Father ever could."

Mrs. Briggs gave her a sympathetic nod. "Indeed 'e would, Caro Angel. Indeed 'e would. Care for a biscuit?"

SHEFFIELD HAD SAID WILL COULD CALL at any time. He'd practically begged him to call and save him from the monotony that would be Ashby House.

How there could be monotony with Miss Perkins about was beyond Will, but he was well aware that he was biased where Miss Perkins was concerned.

Anyone would be.

Will paused as he disembarked from his coach, his eyes widening. What if Sheffield was also biased? The man was living in the same house as her for the time being, and she was the most beautiful creature God's hands had ever created. If heaven had angels with auras of glory, none could be fairer than she.

Why wouldn't Sheffield want such a woman for a wife? She was also witty and capable, not easily ruffled, and far and away the least silly woman Will had ever encountered. She wanted a quiet, simple life, which meant she would never stray, would never ask for much, and was quite likely to always be content so long as care was given her.

Perfection in a woman, he had no doubt.

Sheffield could not have her.

Will's brow snapped down and he strode for Ashby House. He would take it up with his friend at this very moment if he had to, even if it meant declaring his intentions prematurely.

He was that convinced of Miss Perkins suiting him.

It was not gentlemanly at all to act in such haste or to be so rash with a friend he'd had for years.

That suited him rather well indeed.

Lady Ashby's intractable butler Fellows greeted him at his arrival and informed him that Mr. Sheffield had gone out on an errand of a personal nature, and that Miss Sheffield was still away at a house party.

Neither of these statements gave Will any discomfort.

"Would you wish to call upon her ladyship and Miss Perkins?" Fellows continued in his perfectly mild and polite tone.

Why, yes. Yes, he would.

"I would dearly love to pay my respects to both," Will informed the man. "But pray, do not interrupt their schedule for me. I will come to them, if you think it permissible."

Fellows smiled a little. "I think her ladyship would have insisted you come to her anyway, sir. The ladies are in the garden. May I show you the way?"

Satisfied he would have gotten what he wished no matter what he'd said, Will nodded and followed Fellows to the back of the house to a lovely, tidy garden. Lady Ashby sat in a chair with her head tipped back, safely ensconced in the shade while Miss Perkins sat beside her, book in hand, her lips moving as she evidently read aloud.

"Mr. Debenham, your ladyship," Fellows intoned when they reached the ladies.

Will bowed by way of greeting. "My lady, Miss Perkins. I hope neither of you consider my coming a disruption to your day. I did not like to pass without paying my respects."

Lady Ashby beamed up at him through the pallor of her expression. "Of course not, Mr. Debenham! We are delighted to have you, are we not, Miss Perkins?"

Miss Perkins, who had risen and curtseyed, now dipped her chin in the most adorable sign of deference ever. "Yes, ma'am. Delighted."

If the color in her cheeks were any indication, that was not a false statement for Miss Perkins, and the thought sent Will's heart soaring.

Control, his mind ordered with some emphasis.

Right. Control. That was not a gentlemanly request, per se, only a human one. He could listen to such an edict.

"Miss Perkins has been indulging me with some reading this morning after her lessons," Lady Ashby told him, indicating her companion gently. "But I do feel that my ears could rest a while. Would you care to show Mr. Debenham about the gardens, Miss Perkins? It would do you good to walk a bit more. Otherwise you risk becoming old before your years as I am."

He couldn't listen, he wouldn't have control, and he would let his heart soar in whatever direction it would and to whatever heights.

Composed as any gentleman ought to be, Will bowed slightly. "If Miss Perkins is willing, I would very much like to see the gardens."

Miss Perkins nodded once and turned to set her book down on the small table beside Lady Ashby before gesturing towards the garden and stepping onto the stone path.

She could have gestured to hell itself and he would have fallen into step beside her.

Neither of them said anything for a moment, though Will glanced at her enough to have started a conversation a dozen or more times. Her golden hair glowed in the sunlight, and she wore no bonnet or covering for her head. Her complexion was mild enough that she would have colored easily in the sun, and the current fashion for a lady was to stay white and smooth in all exposed skin.

Miss Perkins did not seem particularly perturbed about that.

Fascinating.

"Ought you not to have a bonnet, Miss Perkins?" Will asked with a smile. "Will Lady Ashby comment if your skin should tan?"

Miss Perkins smiled and lifted her eyes to his. "No doubt she would, though she also has said I am too pale. Today she is content to have me go without, and I am content to agree." She tilted her head back, shut her eyes, and exhaled as beams of fortunate sunlight graced her cheeks. "Quite content indeed."

So was he, but Will wasn't going to express such things.

He also exhaled, in an attempt to regain his senses, and managed a polite smile to match hers. "I would think the relative solitude of the house at present would also add to your contentment."

Miss Perkins' eyes snapped open and latched onto his, wide with worry.

His polite smile became something far more mischievous. "Am I wrong?"

Her panic eased and she glanced back at Lady Ashby before replying, "No, you are not, but you mustn't ever say so."

"I would never," he vowed, "though I have no qualms in admitting that I was more than content to call with that solitude in mind."

Miss Perkins clamped down on her perfect lips hard. "You should not say such things, Mr. Debenham," she murmured, though she smiled as she said it.

"I said nothing to offend anyone," he pointed out. "Only an appreciation for the solitude."

"Hmm." Miss Perkins glanced at him, her smile more serene now. "I very much appreciate solitude myself. I find it often with Lady Ashby when it is the pair of us. We may read together, or she may listen to the music I play, and if we do not have engagements, I am permitted so much time to myself. Quite a leisurely thing, when I have completed my lessons."

Will frowned at that, his hands clasping behind his back. "You've mentioned lessons before, Miss Perkins. What lessons are these? I understood from Sheffield that you had finished your education prior to your arrival."

Miss Perkins released a sigh that seemed to carry a great deal in it. "So had I, to be sure. I understood that in order to be best suited for the society that Lady Ashby moves in, I would need additional refinement, but I had no idea that I must be retrained in dancing, elocution, and manners, for I apparently lack education in all of them, despite previous lessons."

"I see no such lack of accomplishment," Will protested, shocked that such a thing would even be considered of a woman of such grace and poise.

"You are kind," came the soft reply. "But Miss Sheffield has assured Lady Ashby and myself that it is so. She has given me an education all her own. I had no idea that blues and greens and stripes and all pink shades were so ill suited to my color and complexion. Or that my fair hair was so very dull. Or that I am paler than death in certain lights."

"I see nothing of the sort," Will overrode in a less than gentlemanly tone, emphasizing each word with great care. "Truly, Miss Perkins, it is not so."

She lifted a slender shoulder in a poor attempt at a careless shrug. "It makes no difference if it is or not. Lady Ashby values the opinion of her niece, and I, as her companion, am in no position to quarrel. I need her patronage in order to gain entry into society. What I wear and how my complexion and hair are fixed makes no difference to me."

Will stared at her in amazement, both at the sentiment she had expressed and the torment that Miss Sheffield had subjected her to. And yet she had borne it all so well, it could hardly be satisfying for the inflictor, who would undoubtedly wish for some reaction.

Miss Perkins did not react.

"Is Miss Sheffield overly concerned with your role here?" Will prodded with as much gentleness as he could manage through the haze of his outrage.

Miss Perkins only nodded. "She is. I think if it were left to her, I would not have been taken on for her ladyship. She disapproves of my being sponsored in exchange. I have recently made the acquaintance of Mrs. and Miss Mayfield. Do you know them?"

"I do, only just."

"Mrs. and Miss Mayfield came to call on me, as they had promised," Miss Perkins went on, her voice as wistful as her gaze, and he dearly wished her gaze would have fallen on him to witness it. "But I was not permitted to see them."

He jerked in shock. "What? When they had called on you?"

Again came the almost shrug. "Miss Sheffield had put it into Lady Ashby's head that it would be inappropriate for a companion to receive guests and callers of such a station." She finally looked at Will, smiling a touch wryly. "Thankfully, Mrs. Mayfield is a stubborn woman with spirit and she said she wished to see me because it was her understanding that I was being sponsored by Lady Ashby in exchange for companionship, and that I was not hired help at all, and how could I possibly hope to succeed in a season even with such a sponsor if I was not permitted to associate with those who could further my influence and standing?"

Will grinned outright, feeling laughter and pride bubble up within him. "How indeed? And have you seen them since?"

"Once," she replied with a nod. "I have also seen my friends from school, but only when we are out."

"Have they called here?" he asked, noting the air of longing he heard.

She shook her head. "No. I have not even told them I am at Ashby House, though they know my situation. I dare say I will see some of them next week at the Radcliffes for the ball." She exhaled in an unreadable manner and looked up at him, apparently also content to change the subject. "Will you go?"

"I will," he vowed, more than agreed. "And I would very much appreciate the first two dances, Miss Perkins, if it is not too bold."

Her progress on the path stopped and she fixed her gaze on a flowering bush nearby. "You don't mind dancing with Lady Ashby's companion?"

Holding his breath, Will reached out and touched her elbow, bringing her dark, beguiling eyes to his. "I would like to dance with Miss Perkins," he told her in a low tone, needing her to understand his meaning perfectly. "I don't care whose companion she may or may not be. The first two, if you please."

Her eyes searched his for a moment, and then, glory of glories, she smiled, the barest flash of white teeth escaping the precious cage of her lips. "That would please me very much, Mr. Debenham. The first two dances are yours."

CHAPTER 8

The Radcliffe ball was just as grand an affair as one might imagine a ball hosted by a viscount and viscountess to be. Miss Sheffield, whose dislike of Caroline did not hinder her from seeing something useful in her, took control of Caroline's wardrobe the moment she returned from the house party. None of the items of clothing aside from the casual everyday wear remained in her room.

Heaven forbid Caroline should steal away in the night and take the gowns with her.

At any rate, this evening she looked well enough. Miss Sheffield had ordered her dressed in a pale blue sprigged muslin that was nearly too tight, but the color was very fine. She had heard from Lady Ashby that with her figure so arrayed, and her hair laced with matching blue ribbon, her dark eyes seemed even more striking. But a pretty dress and almost pretty eyes did not make up for being a daughter of a tradesman, and there were several men, upon hearing her name, who would look at her, smile, and then turn away.

Miss Sheffield's friends were not deterred from such, and, after seeing Lady Ashby comfortably to a chair near a window, at her request, they made a game of introducing Caroline to nearly everyone in attendance. All for the sake of finding her a potential husband that would meet their approval. None of them said anything about *her* approval, but it was apparently a small detail.

Despite it all, Caroline made some very good conversation with people that only months ago would have terrified her. Surprisingly, there were some kind and intelligent members of Society, though very few also possessed the sanity of ignoring the unfortunate circumstances of birth into a trade family. Time would only tell if the dancing for the evening would include the same sort of pattern. She had promised the first two dances to Mr. Debenham, though she had not seen him arrive as yet, though she would not hold him to it, should he wish to change his mind. Nor would she expect to dance any more than that this evening.

Music began and space opened up in the middle of the ballroom for couples.

Caroline held her breath and waited, wondering where the flash of hope had come from. She hadn't hoped for much in her life, but now…

"Miss Perkins."

A rush of breath escaped in an exhale as she turned to see Mr. Debenham coming to her, a faint smile on his handsome face. He bowed perfectly before her, his dark hair darker despite the resplendent number of candles in the room. When his green eyes clashed with hers, and he extended a hand towards her, Caroline swore her knees would give way, though they were as stable as ever.

"The first two dances, I believe," Mr. Debenham said, still smiling.

Caroline put her trembling hand in his, the gloves between them doing nothing at all to dampen the heat between them. "Yes, sir. As I understand it."

His hand closed around hers, and a similar pressure squeezed about her heart. "Then we had best be about it." He led her out to the center with the other couples, lining up in the proper formation.

Caroline's heart pounded furiously within her, though nerves about the dance itself had nothing at all to do with it. It was the man standing across from her, staring with an intensity that tickled something deep inside of her. Something she could not explain or express, and something had never in her life expected.

Dancing with him was beyond anything. He was a graceful dancer, despite rarely being seen to do so, and he put her at ease at once. They had a little conversation, none of which she could later recall. The only thing that remained in her mind was the look in his eyes, which were trained on her the entire dance.

For her part, it was impossible to look anywhere but at him.

The touch of his hand awoke whatever part of her it landed on, be it her waist, her hand, or brushing against her hip on a particularly close pass between them. So many sensations and ripples cascading through her, and she was to dance a second with him?

Surviving that would be a triumph all its own.

"Would it be too much flattery, Miss Perkins," Mr. Debenham asked as the first dance finished and they prepared for the second, "to tell you that you are a picture of loveliness this evening?"

"It would, yes," Caroline murmured, her cheeks feeling warmer than she could ever recall.

He nodded once. "Then I shall not say so."

She bit down her lip, the urge to giggle rising. She never laughed, but with him, she found herself tempted.

If that were not a sign of something significant, she could not say what was.

"You seem a trifle more comfortable than the last time we danced," Mr. Debenham mentioned as the next dance commenced. "Though not altogether quite at ease."

"I feel as though everyone is staring," Caroline admitted freely. "I am all dressed up and giving an impression of finery that does not suit. Everyone knows what I am, and yet they look."

"Let them look," he insisted as he passed her. "Let them see. Some of us are fortunate enough to see you for who you are, not what. And who you are puts what you are quite to shame, not that the what matters at all. Take yourself on the whole, Miss Perkins, not as your parts. Believe me, the whole is stunning in the extreme."

Her breath vanished in its entirety at that, and she could not manage another word throughout the dance. She could only look at him, stare in wonder and delight. Yet she knew full well her path lay along another course than his. A tradesman's daughter from the docks could not do for a man like him. Still, it was heavenly to dream for a while.

She had so little experience with doing so.

The feelings she had for Mr. Debenham were becoming more and more something other than respect, something far deeper and less easy to define. And she could not pretend that there was nothing on his side, though she could certainly doubt it anything but kindness.

Yet those rare smiles of his, when directed at her, the sincerity in his eyes when he looked at her, the honor and respect that she felt from him, all led her to hold him in the highest regard. And her heart, traitorous thing, was beginning to melt a little more and more with every look.

Soon enough, and yet all too soon, the dance was over. Mr. Debenham returned her to her previous position and smiled as he bowed his farewell, though he didn't say a word.

Caroline watched him go, unable to complete a full thought. There was too much she felt, and too much she did not understand.

"Miss Perkins!" came the cheery voice of a young woman. "I was hoping to see you tonight!"

She turned to see Kate Mayfield coming to her, the girl looking the perfect vision of a young Society miss. She would not want for dance partners tonight, if Caroline was any judge.

Not that was particularly experienced in these matters.

"Have you danced yet?" Miss Mayfield asked, her eyes bright with excitement. "I do hope so, it would be such a shame if you did not."

Caroline nodded as she smiled at the younger woman. "I have, yes. Do you hope to dance as well?"

Miss Mayfield nodded eagerly. "I have been practicing all week. I love to dance, when there are partners enough to get a chance."

"Why would you not have a chance?" Caroline queried with a frown. "You're a lovely girl, and a pretty one as well."

"You are kind." Miss Mayfield dipped her chin modestly. "But I lack the open temperament desired by Society. I am told it can be off-putting."

Caroline nearly smiled at that. She was far more reserved than was ideal, and she understood the sentiment all too well. She had never particularly wished to dance, but she had also not been raised in a situation where that might be encouraged.

A pity that Miss Mayfield would likely not have much of a chance to dance this evening, especially if she remained near Caroline. No one had approached her since Mr. Debenham had left, and the ladies who had been so devoted to introducing her to potential partners were now dancing themselves. With the way other guests were skirting around them, and more particularly Caroline, it grew uncomfortable to simply stand there and wait. Neither she nor Miss Mayfield were prone to much talking, so they stood in almost near silence.

Thankfully, Mr. Gates danced soon approached and offered for a dance with Miss Mayfield, so she did not suffer for Caroline's lack of popularity. She might have been mistaken, but Caroline thought she saw a spark of attraction there.

That would be well done indeed. Mr. Gates was very intelligent and witty, spoke his mind plainly, but with respect, and had been very sincere in his regards with Caroline. He, at least, saw her as a person and not a project. Her background did not deter him from kindness or friendship, though he would never see her as a prospect, and nor would she wish him to. But she would be quite content with his apparent pursuit of Miss Mayfield, should it be the case.

After their dance, Mr. Gates took Miss Mayfield elsewhere, making excellent introductions for her, but leaving Caroline to stand there alone.

Several dances passed without her taking part, and Caroline found herself edging closer and closer to the chairs where Lady Ashby and the other women of a certain age or constitution. It would have been lovely to sit among them and listen to their conversation or to simply watch the dancing and enjoy the music. Standing about without friends to associate with or partners to dance with left her feeling exposed and somehow lacking.

"Caroline?"

She whirled to face the voice, her jaw dropping when she saw Penelope approaching, her eyes bright. "Penelope?"

They hugged quickly, and Penelope pulled back to look her over. "Oh, Caroline, you look so lovely! What a perfect gown for you! Of course, you look lovely in anything…"

"Are the others here, too?" Caroline asked, suddenly eager to see the rest of them.

Penelope's shoulder slumped. "Not that I can see. I'm not sure Addy is in London yet, and Jo…"

"Miss Perkins, I was just coming to find you," came the tight voice of Miss Sheffield, and, for the first time, Caroline could have shrieked at her.

She only knew a handful of people that would bring her joy to see, and Penelope was one of them. Now she would be interrupted from spending time with her? But Caroline was well-behaved, as always, and turned with a smile. "Miss Sheffield, may I present my friend, Miss Foster? Penelope, this is Miss Sheffield, Lady Ashby's niece."

Miss Sheffield eyed Penelope speculatively from the tips of her rich black hair to her pristine slippers, and it was clear she doubted the two of them could be friends. Still, she curtseyed politely. "A pleasure, Miss Foster. And how do you know our Miss Perkins?"

Penelope quirked a brow. "She is one of my best friends from school, Miss Sheffield. We were together at Miss Bell's, and I am very fond of her, indeed."

Caroline knew that tone in Penelope, and bit the inside of her lip, unsure if she were delighted at hearing it or terrified.

"And are you in London for the Season, Miss Foster?" Miss Sheffield asked in her too-superior tone.

Caroline almost shook her head in warning at Miss Sheffield, but decided, ultimately, to let Penelope do as she would. After all, she was no fool.

Penelope smirked in the way that only Penelope could. "I am, Miss

Sheffield, and in the care of my guardian, the Duke of Blackbourne. I intend to take every advantage I can of the Season, and particularly wish to encourage my friends to do the same."

Miss Sheffield's eyes widened at the same rate as the color faded from her cheeks. She swallowed twice, then managed a weak smile. "Of course, of course." She turned the smile to Caroline. "Would you be a dear, Caroline, and find my aunt? She was asking for you earlier and would not tell me what she wished. You are so dear to her, you know, and she only trusts you."

Lady Ashby did no such thing, fond as she was of Caroline, and no one in the entire house called her by her given name. What a game Miss Sheffield was playing for Penelope. No doubt she would question her mercilessly on the subject of the duke, who was unmarried, and see what sort of advantage she could make from Caroline's connection to Penelope.

"Of course," Caroline murmured, going along with the game. She turned to Penelope, who looked less than pleased. "If I do not see you later, I will send you a note."

"I look forward to it," Penelope replied through clenched teeth.

Caroline mouthed an apology once Miss Sheffield turned back to Penelope, and then made her way to Lady Ashby, who needed nothing.

Not wishing to rejoin Miss Sheffield for anything, Caroline merely stood by and watched the dancing again.

Miss Smythe and Miss Fairchild joined Caroline in short order and were rather put out that she had not been swarmed by partners, though Miss Sheffield, who eventually joined them, to Caroline's dismay, did not appear surprised at all. Mr. Jacobs and Mr. Rhoades roamed about the room and flirted shamelessly, dancing grandly and with much enthusiasm with any woman who would give them the slightest attention. Miss Sheffield herself was a very popular partner for the dance, and she did not restrain her triumphant smile every time.

Caroline did not dance at all for the next hour, though all of the other ladies did, and she could not escape to go back to Penelope, as she was almost always engaged in conversation with someone, though her actual participation in the conversation was stilted at best.

Then, quite shockingly, Mr. Debenham approached and asked Caroline to dance for a third time. Miss Sheffield gasped, but she could hardly scold her dear Deb in front of everyone at the ball.

Caroline accepted, of course, and again, almost quivered as he led her out. Miss Smythe had been speaking of Mr. Debenham incessantly, and now Caroline's mind whirled with newfound knowledge, useless though it was for dancing with him. He was not a particularly powerful man of Society or anything so popular, but he was from a good family and had ties to a powerful set of relatives whose circle was in London. He had a very attractive fortune, an enviable country estate, and was the epitome of gentleman. As far as Miss Smythe knew, the only reason he had not married as yet was because no woman was good enough for him.

It sounded rather superior or selective, but Caroline could not think that Mr. Debenham's particular wishes in a wife would be something impossible to attain. He was such a kind, warm man, and so comfortable to be with, despite his reserve. Surely it would not be so impossible to be his wife.

No, indeed, as she caught her breath looking at him, she thought it might be rather lovely to be the wife of such a man. But what did he wish for? What did he expect? With such family ties to be had in Society, was he as free as he liked? Did he have duties to fulfill?

What did he think of *her* in truth?

"What do you see that makes you appear so thoughtful, I wonder," Mr. Debenham mused as he took her hand to lead her around the nearest couple.

Caroline swallowed hard. "Only more questions, Mr. Debenham."

"Anything I could give answers to?" he asked.

She shook her head, not trusting herself to be bold. "I do not have the intrepid nature enough to even ask them, sir."

Mr. Debenham squeezed her hand tightly as he moved her through the final motions. "I would happily answer any question you asked me. Any at all."

"I cannot ask," she whispered, her throat going instantly raw.

The pressure at her hand increased for just a moment, the pressure racing into her chest. "Someday, Miss Perkins, I pray that you will."

"When I asked you to call upon us regularly, I didn't intend for you to come daily."

Will glanced over at Sheffield as his friend lounged in one of the chairs in the study. "I have not come daily."

That earned him a derogatory glower. "Would I have said you had if you had not?"

"Probably, yes."

Sheffield considered that, then nodded. "Point taken, however..." He held up a finger, then leveled it at Will. "You have been remarkably attentive to us, and I don't believe it is due to your affection for me."

Will smiled very tightly. "Fond as I am of you, Sheffield, you are correct."

His friend gestured as if that were obvious. "Care to share?"

"No."

Now Sheffield looked more disgruntled than anything else. "Deb, it's just us. Gates, Jacobs, and Rhoades will be in here any moment, and then we'll have to join the ladies. You cannot expect me to remain silent."

"I can, and I do." Will shrugged and folded his hands together. "I have nothing to tell, not even to you."

And the truth of it was, he wouldn't have had anything to tell anyone else either. What could he say? That his mind utterly refused to dwell on any subject other than that of Miss Perkins? That he was actively seeking additional invitations to balls just for the chance to dance with her again? That his feet knew the path to Ashby House better than he could ever admit?

All of those things were true; what it meant was far less clear.

He could have claimed he was in love with Miss Perkins, but it wouldn't have been entirely true. He *could* be in love with Miss

Perkins, but he wouldn't extend to that extreme yet. He *wanted* to be in love with Miss Perkins, but her reserve gave him pause.

It wasn't a hindrance, it only made things less clear.

He adored her reserve. He found deciphering her expression a challenge impossible to resist. He could have devoted his entire life to the pursuit of making her smile.

And he would have died a contented man to hear her laugh only once.

Ideally, he would hear it more than once, and several times at that, but once would be enough.

He could very easily love Miss Perkins. He just wasn't sure he was prepared to.

Will Debenham had never been in love before, but if it was as tossed about as he had been for the past few weeks, he understood the rush to Gretna Green so many couples undertook.

What was a mad jaunt of an elopement in the face of an equally mad future?

Miss Perkins would never have gone off to Gretna Green.

Alas for his attempts at less gentlemanly behavior.

Aside from all of that, Will wasn't sure he trusted Sheffield where Miss Perkins was concerned either. After Will had danced with Miss Perkins a third time, she had danced with Sheffield, which peeved his sister greatly.

Will could approve of that, even if he glared at Sheffield the entire dance.

A few other gentlemen approached her after that, apparently nonplussed by her fortune in trade, despite the inanity of the other gentlemen in the room. The woman was a beauty of unrivaled proportions, and yet she had stood about like a spinster most of the night. He would never understand Society, he was sure of it.

Will had watched each of the dances with interest, and none were anything to be considered a success, by the standards of their group. Yet it could certainly have been, enough to give her some hope at securing a match in the future. Mr. Clarke, in particular, had Will concerned. He was a curate in Cheshire, Will had discovered, and the man was in London visiting his cousins. He had treated Miss Perkins with the respect and deference she deserved.

He could only hope that Clarke was lacking in wit and spark, and that he perpetually smelled of brandy.

But even if that had been the case, Miss Perkins might not have minded. She was such a different sort of creature, so calm in demeanor and tranquil in manner. She was above and beyond the other women of his association, and certainly of their present party. She was rare, and she was perfect.

Perfection. Exactly what the proper gentleman would want in a wife.

Pity.

"Sheffield, Debenham!" one of the other men called. "We're going to the music room with the ladies!"

Will rolled his eyes up to the ceiling. "And these are the men your sister chose to adopt into her circle?"

Sheffield shrugged as he rose from his chair. "Gates isn't so bad. And the Season isn't forever."

No, it was not forever, but it was certainly long enough.

The music room wasn't particularly grand, but it would suit the group for now, although he wasn't quite sure why they had chosen the music room unless the ladies were going to perform.

He prayed not.

"Miss Perkins, will you play for us so that we might dance?" Miss Fairchild asked before any of them could get settled. "I have the mad desire to dance!"

Will could have groaned. If he was going to dance, he wanted to dance with the woman playing not with the rest. But he was, unfortunately, a gentleman, so dance he would.

"Yes, Miss Perkins, you must play," Miss Sheffield insisted in a stern tone. "A lady must play in public for her talent to be considered real accomplishment. Off you go."

There was certainly no cause for that sort of behavior, but Miss Perkins did as she was bid, as she usually did.

As it happened, she played rather well. Better than he had expected with her reserve and her background, but Miss Perkins would ever be a surprise, it seemed. And what a delightful surprise she was.

The company danced quite a few dances, and Lady Ashby seemed to delight in them all. Miss Perkins did not seem to tire in the slightest, and her music was consistently perfect.

But of course it was.

"Come, Miss Perkins," Gates said as they finished yet another dance. "Miss Smythe can take a turn at the instrument while you dance. And I'll not hear a word of protest, for even a future wife of a curate must dance once or twice, if a curate is still your preference."

Good fellow, Will thought with some respect, though he wished the notion had been his own. He glanced around the room and noticed that Miss Sheffield, for one, looked fairly ready to shriek.

He would let Gates dance with Miss Perkins all night if it would render that reaction.

"I am afraid that I am quite fatigued," Lady Ashby sighed from her chair. "Don't let me stop you from your enjoyment, but I must retire."

"Of course, my lady," Miss Perkins replied immediately, rushing from the instrument as though she had been saved from danger. "I will take you upstairs and read for you."

"Well, why not do your reading down here, Aunt?" Sheffield suggested with his usual warm joviality. "None of us will mind a reprieve, and it will keep both you and Miss Perkins with us a bit longer."

The group all sounded their agreement and approval of the suggestion, though Miss Perkins looked rather as if she wished the floor would swallow her whole.

"Oh, very well," Lady Ashby sighed. "Have my copy of John Donne fetched, and Miss Perkins may favor the company with a poem."

The book was fetched, Miss Perkins situated, and from the moment she began to read, Will was sunk.

Her voice, low and without airs, seemed too perfectly situated to the words, and her careful attention to each word forced their attention to the content of the poem as well as her presentation of it. What exactly she was saying, he couldn't recall, as his attention was too wrapped up in the experience for comprehension.

"'If our two loves be one, or, thou and I/Love so alike, that none do slacken, none can die.'" Miss Perkins closed the book with a faint exhale, and kept her eyes cast down as though awaiting their judgment.

What judgment could there possibly be for something so lovely?

"I say, Miss Perkins," Mr. Jacobs said then, sounding rather impressed, "you do the thing properly, don't you?"

"She certainly does," Sheffield replied in the same.

Will found both comments lacking but said nothing.

"I will never be so gifted," Miss Fairchild bemoaned, drawing attention back to herself as the men assured her of her many talents.

Miss Sheffield, Will noticed, watched Miss Perkins with an unreadable expression, but her eyes held a suspicious sheen. "Miss Perkins take my aunt to bed," she suddenly snapped. "Can you not see that she is most fatigued?"

"I am well enough," Lady Ashby sighed. "I was lulled by dear Caroline here and quite comfortable. But now it would be lovely to rest, if you do not mind, my dear." She extended her hand to her nephew, who helped her to rise.

Miss Perkins smiled at her patroness. "Of course, my lady."

Will moved the moment she went to set the book aside, his hand extended to take the book and assist her

She looked up at him in confusion as she handed the book to him. "Thank you."

"No," he replied simply, words escaping him. "Thank you." Then he smiled at her. "You are full of secrets and surprises, are you not?"

"No," she insisted, her cheeks heating. "I am not."

Will could have grinned, the heat of her cheeks giving him hope. "You are." He leaned a bit closer as he helped her rise, though she needed no aid. "Is Caroline your real name?"

Her eyes darted to his. "I…"

"Caroline, darling, don't forget your wrap," Lady Ashby said, soundly half asleep.

Miss Perkins jerked her hand from his and twisted to get her wrap, but he had already grabbed it and draped it around her. He took the briefest moment of indulgence to adjust the wrap, his fingers brushing against her arms and her back as he did so.

She was still as he fiddled with it, though her breathing did not seem entirely steady.

"There," he murmured, wishing to the heavens that they were alone.

As if she nodded, Miss Perkins stepped forward to take Lady Ashby from Sheffield, who smiled with warmth, but not adoration, much to Will's delight. Miss Perkins did not look at Will as they left the room, and somehow, he knew she would not rejoin them once her charge was settled.

He did not mind that as much as he thought he would. He was content for the night.

Her name was Caroline.

And he was in love with her.

CHAPTER 9

*C*aroline sat quietly at the pianoforte, her fingers absently playing in whatever semblance of melodies and harmonies they wished, no structure or form to any of it. But it was full of feeling and it soothed the turmoil and confusion within her. Music had always been able to do so for her, even when she had only been able to play on the tinny instrument that had sat in the corner of their house on the docks. Her attempts had been far less musical then, but the soothing had been the same.

She was in desperate need of soothing now.

Not for anything particularly troublesome, or discouraging, but simply due to the feelings that had begun to course through her at the mere thought of Mr. Debenham.

She had never felt anything like it, her experience with men being limited to her father's employees and the other men at the docks, and occasionally the parents or brothers of her friends. She had never even had the girlish rush of impossible romance for someone she could never have. Caroline Perkins had always been far too sensible for anything of the sort, even as a child.

It seemed she would be making up for that deficit now, and with compound interest. Mr. Debenham was certainly not the simple country curate she had imagined for herself, but he possessed the gentle and good nature she had always wanted. He was intelligent and considerate, reserved without being aloof, and he seemed to miss nothing in his observations. He was handsome enough to warrant a second or third look every time she saw him, not that such things mattered.

The only thing she could say to his detriment was that he did not see her as she truly was, but that could only be due to his kindness.

He was also impossibly above her in station, fortune, in manner, and in every way that mattered. She might have had the respectable dowry of any woman in Society, but she was a tradesman's daughter. And not even a respectable one at that,

Dreaming and thinking of him would only lead to her anguish later. It would be best for all concerned if she would forget him and focus instead on finding herself a husband more within her reach.

But how to forget Mr. Debenham at all?

This was the song her heart and fingers played, and she waited in vain for its resolution.

"Miss Perkins," Fellows intoned rather stiffly from the door of the room. "You have a... a visitor."

Caroline frowned over at him. "A visitor? For me?"

Fellows looked at her with distaste. "Indeed." He inclined his head, and stood back, letting the visitor proceed in.

From the first sight, Caroline's heart plummeted into her stomach. Her father.

He wavered into the room, barely able to walk straight, and the stained and faded linen shirt he wore under his tattered blue coat told everyone who would see him exactly where he belonged by station.

"Caro!" he cried, extending his arms out as if to hug her, though she had yet to rise, and he was still a distance away.

Her lack of reaction disgruntled him, and his thick, bushy brows snapped down. He pointed a finger at her as he approached. "Don't 'ee give me that look. I still be your father, and t' Bible says 'ee honor me."

Caroline was convinced that her father had never read a single word of scripture in his life, but she could not fault the statement. She rose and bobbed the barest hint of a curtsey. "Papa."

He grunted without satisfaction. "Caroline, you're being disloyal to your old man," he said, leaning against the pianoforte, which made her wince. He was so dirty and disheveled he was sure to leave traces on the instrument that she would have to clean later.

"How so, Papa?" she replied as calmly as she could, lacing her fingers before her.

He glared at her through his bloodshot eyes, no affection in his gaze. "'Ee have grown so high and mighty, so proper, so full of the airs of a class to which you don't belong, that you refuse to help me. I'm on hard times, Chickee, and you ignore my letters!"

Caroline shook her head, "I have not ignored anything."

"Don't shake 'ee head at me, you tart!" he scolded, staggering towards her. "I never saw one letter from you! And I know you've been writing Coolidge!"

She bit her lip and tried to look sympathetic. "I wanted to know how bad it was," she whispered. "I needed to know the truth."

"Then you should have written to me about it!" Her father began to pace around awkwardly, his steps uneven and faltering. "And 'ee can't even spare some of your salary to save us."

"I write to 'ee all the time," she said, not even caring that her old accent was running rampant. "Do 'ee know how hard it is to get a letter sent to 'ee from where I am now? Do you know how worried I have been?"

"Not worried enough, Chickee," he said with a cold laugh. "Not by half."

His voice had grown so harsh, so dark and unlike the man she knew as her father, that Caroline had to grip the edge of the instrument to steel herself.

"It is not my fault you haven't seen the letters," she said firmly, trying to regain the accent she had trained for. "Ask Mrs. Briggs or Mr. Coolidge if you can't see them. And I have no coin to give you. I don't earn salary, I've told you! I'm no' a servant to Lady Ashby. All I have is pin money."

"Then get that!" he barked. "Get it or, so help me, Caroline Perkins…"

"So help you what?" she demanded, lifting her chin, quivering despite her tone. "You'll cut me off? You'll take back your permission? You can't cut me off, Papa, I know how my fortune works. And your permission means nothing anymore, because I have friends and connections."

He laughed harshly. "Friends? 'Ee think any of these toffs are interested in a ladder climbing guttersnipe? 'Ee are a plaything for the con… for the condescen…. for the pity of the vacant minded rich!"

"Says the man wasting his life away on drink and whores," she shot back.

Before she knew what happened, Caroline's father slapped her across the face with so much force she tumbled to the floor.

"Pay me, Caro!" he screamed. "Pay me or lose me!"

Rage unlike anything Caroline had ever known surged within her, and she turned to face him, getting to her feet, one hand at her stinging cheek. She glared at her father, eyes watering. "No' one penny," she rasped, feeling strangled by the words. "No' a bleeding one. No' ever."

He snarled and moved to strike her again, but something changed in his eyes. "I knew it," he hissed, shaking his head. "'Ee cannot be a daughter of mine. Paul's little brat got by my wife. No flesh and blood o' mine. 'Ee be nothing t'me, Caro. Nothing." He sniffed noisily and turned from the room.

Caroline sank onto the bench as her knees gave out, breath rushing from her lungs. She knew that her father could not prove any illegitimacy, but his accusation wounded as much as the blow had. She exhaled again, closing her eyes, praying for strength.

"What in the world was all that about?" came the calm and quiet voice she had come to love so much.

Oh, her humiliation could not be more compounded than at this moment, and she raised her eyes to see Mr. Debenham coming into the room. Thankfully, she had not cried, and her tears remained contained.

She could not do this. She would not. "Nothing to trouble you, Mr. Debenham," she murmured, rising to go.

He waved his hand for her to remain and tilted his head at her. "Miss Perkins…"

"Caroline," she whispered, sinking back down, fatigued by the whole charade now.

He nodded. "Caroline, then. I know it was your father. I heard everything."

"You were listening?" she managed, mortification and shame washing over her in succeeding waves.

He shook his head slowly. "Not by intention, Caroline. I would never invade your privacy, you know this. But neither of you were keeping your voices down."

Caroline covered her face and groaned. "Oh, you heard how I speak. You heard my harshness towards him."

"That is what is troubling you?" he asked, sounding surprised. He took her wrists gently in his hold and pulled her hands away from her face, crouching down before her. "I barely noticed that. Caroline, he threatened you. And…" His jaw tightened as he saw the mark on her face. "And he hit you. Does this happen often?"

She shook her head, swallowing. "Never," she whispered. "He's never been like this. But I couldn't give into him. I won't." She exhaled slowly and nodded firmly to herself, steeling her resolve.

Mr. Debenham smiled and shook his head. "Does anything get to you, Caroline Perkins?"

Caroline reared back a little in surprise. "Of course, it does."

His smile grew and his hold on her seemed to warm a little. "You are always so calm, so stalwart, so unaffected. You possess an unnatural serenity."

She laughed once and gave him a look. "You heard me screeching at my father just now, Mr. Debenham. Hardly serene."

"Will," he said softly. "And you are as serene as the dawn."

Caroline tried not to sigh, but it was fruitless. "I am as emotional and human as the rest of the world. I simply contain it until I can be alone."

"And then?" he prodded.

She was desperate to look into his eyes but knew she would be lost if she did so. She focused instead on their hands, shrugging as she turned her hands within his hold, feeling the skin brush together. "I have found there is comfort and strength in tears."

His grip on her hands tightened and his expression turned earnest. "You should not have to bear it alone."

Caroline slowly, reluctantly, slid her hands from his and settled them in her lap. "How else can I? The ground on which I tread is tenuous at best. I do not mind being alone with my emotions. I prefer it, in fact."

He straightened, shaking his head slowly. "I don't prefer it. Not for you, I don't."

"It is far more ladylike, I can assure you." She rose and moved past him, averting her eyes, suddenly uncomfortable. "I pray you never find me emotional."

"And I shall pray I do," he murmured. "Comforting you would be such a pleasure for me. Not to see you in distress, but to be the one with you as you endure it."

She couldn't bear this, couldn't bear the picture he had painted in her mind. Her heart ached for it, longed for his arms around her, but her mind knew far better. She closed her eyes and clamped her lips together. "Good day, Mr. Debenham."

"It's Will, Caroline."

Will. His name caught in her mind and swirled through every memory she treasured of him.

Still she shook her head. "No," she whispered, not knowing if he heard her. "No, it's not. It can't be."

She strode from the room, her heart fair breaking within her chest. How could he be so kind and generous after what he had witnessed? It was impossible to comprehend, and even more impossible to dwell on. What was worse was that he would not abandon her while their association continued. She knew him too well, he would always be this same gentleman, despite everything.

It would hurt all the more to have him so. She could almost wish he would leave her entirely alone.

But that thought hurt most of all.

If WILL DEBENHAM were a less than perfect gentleman, he would have thrashed Caroline Perkins' father to within an inch of his life for the way he had spoken to her, let alone striking her. It had taken every ounce of his good breeding and manners to restrain himself from bursting in and coming to her defense, and had he known that her being struck was a risk, he *would* have been in the room with her.

But alas, he was a perfect gentleman and he hadn't known.

And the love he felt for Caroline grew beyond limits he thought possible after that morning.

The days following had found her more reserved than she had been, more attentive to Lady Ashby than was necessary, and more inclined to make her invisible to all others in the room. It would never entirely work, she was far too beautiful a creature to ignore, but she was reserved enough that it would have been simple enough to forget to include her in conversation.

Gates and Sheffield did their best to bring her into discussions, and Miss Dawson made it a point to sit near her at every opportunity, but Caroline herself did nothing to encourage them.

Miss Sheffield and the others were content enough to leave her be, forgoing even their customary teasing and husband planning. Lady Ashby spoke with Caroline as often as any woman does with her companion, but always in low tones that Will could not politely overhear.

He could not bear to see Caroline making herself into less than she was. He knew that she saw herself far beneath her company, and he would have moved heaven and earth to change that for her. Couldn't she see that her birth and where her fortune came from made absolutely no difference to him? He wasn't naive enough to think everyone felt the same way, and he could even say that he almost understood why members of society avoided her in social gatherings.

He didn't agree with them, but he understood.

And now he was in a carriage rattling along with Sheffield and Gates, headed for a house party in the country in the middle of the Season. He couldn't begin to understand how Sheffield managed to get them all invitations when only Lady Ashby and her companion had been invited, but he would be eternally grateful.

The whole party had been invited, which Miss Sheffield was mildly irritated by, it seemed. She could not bear the thought of being away from the bustle of the true London Season, and the only reason she was attending was the chance that there might be some opportunities for good connections for her there. If she had wanted to rusticate in the country, she declared, she would have stayed in Yorkshire. Miss Smythe and Miss Fairchild agreed but came along for support. Jacobs and Rhoades loved the idea of country pursuits and country misses, so they needed little encouragement.

Will was likely the only one positively thrilled by this venture.

The Mayfields had decided that their daughter would be more comfortable in a less intimidating setting in society, so their cousins, Lord and Lady Mayfield, had opened up their sprawling Richmond estate just outside of London. It was, they declared, in close enough proximity to London that anyone wishing to make the journey back for events would be able to do so, but far enough removed that those wishing for more solitude would have it.

Solitude and the country, and Caroline Perkins.

He needed nothing else.

If only he could get her to see herself as he did.

But that, he feared, would take a lifetime of effort. One that he was more than willing to offer her.

If he thought she would accept, he would have offered.

Not yet. She needed time, and he had time to give. He could convince her of his sincerity and her worth. Gentleman or no gentleman, he knew he had that ability. Caroline would not be won over by charm, by fortune, or by anything else that he had learned to expect from a young woman.

That alone gave him hope.

He could be the man that she wanted for her future, if she would let him.

"You're far away," Sheffield murmured as he roused himself from his dozing against the carriage wall.

Will smiled to himself. "I am in the past, the present, and the future, I think. All three, but it makes my head pain something fierce."

"Sounds intense in my mind." Sheffield adjusted his position and eyed him carefully. "You weren't particularly in the mood to share earlier, has that changed?"

"I'm not entirely sure." Will made a face. "You'll likely think I'm as mad as you did when I said I wanted to be less of a gentleman."

Sheffield nodded once. "More than likely. Well, then I'll confide in you and see what you think."

Oh good. Will restrained a not-quite irritated sigh, rather wishing for his solitude back.

"I find myself in a bit of a predicament," Sheffield informed him in a calm, unaffected voice. "One that could have drastic repercussions for my life."

"Sounds uncomfortable," Will replied, feeling that absent replies on his part might give the impression that he was actually listening and engaged in this conversation.

"It is, to be sure." Sheffield gazed out of the window as they rolled towards Richmond. "You see, I have found myself drawn more and more to a young woman of my acquaintance. She is loveliness itself, defies anything I ever thought I would find in my life, and I think nothing would make me happier than to have her as my wife."

Slowly Will felt his heart pounding its way down to the pit of his stomach. He blinked at his friend, who was not giving him any consideration at all for the moment. "So... will you offer for her?" he barely forced out.

Sheffield shook his head, his attention still on the window. "Not yet. There are too many obstacles to consider, and I must work them all out in my mind."

He had never heard of Sheffield having particular affection for any woman, let alone one with obstacles. It did not take him long to draw up a list of potential candidates for Sheffield's affections, and he needed to narrow it down.

For his own sanity.

"What obstacles?" Will asked his friend, keeping his tone careful and bored. "You're a decently wealthy man from a respectable family, and you have some manners, when you choose to employ them."

That earned Will a mocking look, and Sheffield laughed once. "The usual obstacles for a man in my situation. Station, fortune, expectations... I risk losing all that I have to follow my heart in this. I cannot say for certain that my parents will approve. I know Anna will not. And my aunt... I have no way of knowing her thoughts on the matter."

Worse and worse. Will exhaled slowly, silently. "Then she is not of fortune herself?"

Sheffield shook his head. "Not immediately, no. A great deal of potential, but differences in station and the views of such..." He looked at Will with some evidence of real despair. "I have not your strength of character, Deb. I am not decided on my course, and I fear that makes me unworthy of her."

"It may," Will said slowly, hoping he could encourage his friend without actually guiding him down the path he greatly feared Sheffield would go down. "But it is also worth your consideration to take in all aspects of the decision. We cannot pretend that marrying for our hearts does not have its drawbacks."

"Far easier to have affection *and* position," Gates murmured from his position, still acting as though he slept. "If you can manage it."

Will and Sheffield looked over at him in some amusement, exchanging wry looks with each other as they did so. "And if one cannot?" Sheffield prodded.

Gates shrugged against the carriage wall, never once opening his eyes. "Then one must simply decide if the drawbacks of marrying such a woman are worth the happiness she might provide."

Trust Gates to be frank about a situation that was not as simple as he made it out to be, and yet strike at the truth of the matter.

Will asked the question he was afraid to. "And if she is?"

Gates opened his eyes at this and looked at Will directly. "Then marry her, of course, and damn the consequences."

"They will say I am unprincipled and unconventional," Sheffield reminded him.

Gates glanced at him. "Then I say to hell with principle and convention." He smiled with some mischief and settled back in for the remainder of the ride. "Though, as I said, it is much easier to manage affection and position. I intend to."

Will and Sheffield looked at each other again, then back to Gates. "Do you?" Sheffield inquired. "With whom, pray tell?"

"You shall know by and by," Gates replied airily.

Well, well, would wonders never cease?

Will hesitated, then looked at Sheffield. "And will you reveal the identity of your love, Sheffield?"

Sheffield returned his look, then smiled slightly. "You shall know by and by," he repeated.

That was not at all comforting.

The man could have described Caroline in his fears, and though Will had never seen him treat Caroline with the sort of love and adoration such sentiments would have brought about, he could not account for how he behaved when the company had left Ashby House.

What if he intended to offer for her? And, horror of horrors, what if she accepted? What if Sheffield found her in her emotional distress after the attack of her father the other day, and *he* was the one to comfort her? What if he, too, knew of the sweetness and strength Caroline possessed and wanted such for his own?

What if Will were not alone in his desires to bring Caroline out of the obscurity she seemed content to dwell in?

"And your thoughts, Deb?" Sheffield asked, bringing him back to the conversation at hand. "Any more inclined to share?"

He could not reveal his thoughts in truth, not to a potential rival for Caroline. He would not.

Will shrugged once. "Trying to decide if being ungentlemanly would truly suit my needs."

"Oh, spare me," Sheffield groaned, raising his eyes heavenward. "How many times must I tell you that it will not?"

Will managed a smile he did not feel, hiding the satisfaction of knowing that the only ungentlemanly thing he wished to do was to marry far beneath his station and be the most unconventional man who had ever earned the name of gentleman.

That was all.

CHAPTER 10

*P*arkway Manor, home of Lord and Lady Mayfield, was a glorious escape from the troubles of London.

Caroline could barely think of her pains over Will Debenham during the day, though they plagued her enough in the evenings and at night. There were so many children about the house from various families also in attendance, which was entirely unusual for house parties in the Season. The Mayfields did not seem to mind, and with Kate Mayfield being so intrigued by Mr. Gates, she had minimal use for Caroline's company. Lady Ashby was so entertained by others, Caroline was free to do as she please, and it pleased her to play with the children whenever permitted.

It was a blessed reprieve from Society's demands. When the children were abed, there was dancing and evening activities she attended, but when possible, she was with the children.

Life was so much simpler for them.

When they were not about and distracting her, the truth of her situation made itself known in all its anguish.

Caroline was in love with Mr. Debenham. She could barely stand to think of him as Will, much as her heart cried out his name in its loneliest moments. She could not bring him to an equal level with her, not when he was so very far above her.

What was worse was that the time at Parkway Manor had only increased her admiration for him. He was constant in his tender attention, never ceasing in his consideration of her, despite the attempts of others to prevent it. Every evening, she struggled to recount to herself what happened within her when he would look at her, when he gave her that slight smile, when he pressed her hand… She thought she might burst into a thousand pieces every evening, and she found herself craving his presence with ever increasing fervency.

There had been five evenings of dancing thus far, and, surprisingly, a number of gentlemen had danced with her. Each man of the Sheffields' friends had danced with her several times, though none so much as Mr. Debenham. He had the unspoken claim on her first and last dances of the evening, and everyone seemed to know it.

Even Caroline knew it. He could have the claim on every one of her dances, if he would ask. And if she would allow it. There was some internal debate as to whether or not she would. It wasn't proper; she wasn't sure that mattered all the time.

Mr. Sheffield had taken care to dance with Caroline at every opportunity as well, but he seemed somehow more reserved and more thoughtful than usual. Mr. Gates continued his apparent pursuit of Kate Mayfield, and it was remarkable to see the change in her. She was no longer a timid little mouse but had blossomed into one of the most sought-after ladies, despite her timidity. Yet she had eyes for only Mr. Gates, and it was a glorious thing to see.

Country life was really more to Caroline's taste. Every morning she was able to rise early and see to Lady Ashby's comfort, though she was never easy in a house that was not her own. Still, she was adjusting well enough. Her friend Lady Whimpole was also at Parkway Manor, which put a certain amount of life into her, and it was delightful for Caroline to see the two of them together throughout the day, giggling as schoolgirls over nothing in particular. But that was generally not until tea time at least, as Lady Whimpole slept a great deal longer than Lady Ashby did, so in the mornings, she had only Caroline. Despite her attempts to be helpful, Caroline had been forbidden to help the maids with the breakfast trays, and could not do anything to tidy up either, leaving her quite at her wit's end before it was proper for them to leave their rooms.

After the breakfast trays had been cleared, Caroline tried to take her ladyship for a stroll out of doors, if the weather was fine, though it was growing too chilly for such things. Caroline did not mind it, but Lady Ashby was not nearly so hardy. On those days, they simply walked from room to room of the Parkway Manor, with Caroline's arm supporting her. She tired too easily, and Caroline feared the strain of such an extensive house party, so far from her comforts of home, was wearing on her.

Miss Sheffield, for all her professing of being so devoted to her aunt, was nowhere to be found unless there were a great many people. She seemed to be avoiding them both and could not look at Caroline without a hint of a snarl. Whatever usefulness she saw in her had faded now she could not ignore her dear Deb's attention to Caroline.

It was impossible to say why Miss Sheffield was so vulgar about it, as he was still as polite and cordial as he had ever been to her. Caroline had not prevented their usual interaction from continuing, and he certainly had showed no serious inclination in her before, but perhaps Miss Sheffield's heart was broken over his lack of romantic interest.

Provided she had a heart.

Caroline winced at her own cruelty. Yet she had heard Miss Dawson say the same thing to Miss Fairchild not two days ago, and Miss Fairchild agreed. Miss Dawson was always so kind to Caroline, and quite encouraging as well. Her maid was generously helping Caroline with her hair and gowns, as well as Miss Dawson's, and Caroline flattered herself that she looked quite well nearly all the time. They had decided, Miss Dawson and herself, to dispense with the attempts at looking finer, as it did not suit Caroline or her nature. Miss Dawson had even claimed that Caroline looked all the more refined for the simple elegance and wondered why she could not see it before.

It seemed that among Miss Sheffield's friends, Caroline might have found one of her own. Such a good, generous creature, and one without current prospects. Perhaps in this house party, she might find her source of happiness as well.

All the more pressing upon Caroline's thoughts was what she must see to when she returned to London. Mr. Clarke, the kind curate from the Radcliffe ball, had written and asked if he might call upon her when she returned. His letter was so polite and had the slightest bit of sentiment to it, which Caroline found quite charming. Truly, she must consider it, for her situation was not suitable for her wishes.

She could not have Mr. Debenham, should he have the poor judgment to pursue the attachment. He was the second son of an earl. A titled family in England could not attach itself to a bankrupt tradesman's daughter, no matter how secure her own holdings were. She had no pedigree and very little to offer.

She must be sensible.

But lord help her, she struggled to see sense anywhere.

Thus Caroline spent as much of her time as possible with the children. There were fourteen children in all, the youngest only three, and they played and romped, and had the merriest of times! She had even begun to slip into her natural accent, and they did not mind at all. She had lost four ribbons, two fichus, and ruined at least three pairs of stockings in her playing. Two days ago, they were caught in the rain, and the younger children struggled to return to the house, so she had carried them in her arms and on her back, and her dress was near to tatters from all of that. Many of the guests were shocked by her appearance, but the children were so merry, she could not find the shame she ought to have.

The looks on their faces were so comical, even now! She might have been stark naked for all of their scandalized looks. Yet the parents of the children in question smiled, and Mr. Debenham... Will... Well, his smile warmed her chilled body quite admirably, and the look in his eyes made her blush from head to frozen toe.

Caroline was not the only one to indulge in child's play at the party. She had seen Will himself play with the children, and they adored him. He might as well have been their favorite uncle, though none of them had known him before the party began. Hardly any of the other guests lowered themselves to entertain the children, but the two of them did. Never together, but somehow, it felt as though they were.

It was impossible to think on such things without imagining how life would be with him should they have married and had children. Caroline had never thought of children beyond the general seeking to be a mother, but when she considered the prospect of Will and how good he was with them, she yearned for their family more than ever. As many children as they wished, all to be loved, adored, and played with every day of their lives.

None of them would know the evils that Caroline had done, nor the shame of her life's secrets. They would only know joy and loyalty, hope and encouragement from the parents, and love between them all.

Always an abundance of love.

Caroline closed her eyes now as she had escaped the parlor with the ladies and gentlemen. She was permitted this every evening now, though at first it had been a secret. She had snuck out one night at the behest of the children to read to them in the library. It was a treat for them before bedtime, and she had the benefit of not being subjected to the endless tittle tattle of adults who had nothing of real substance to say. They were all very good people, it was true, but Caroline knew so little of them and their society, it made her discomfort too great.

She remained in the parlor as long as she must to see to Lady Ashby, and once the lady was settled and comfortable, was away to the library where the children waited.

Of course, after the first night of reading stories from a collection of fairy tales, and naturally doing all of the voices, the delighted children informed their parents. Thankfully, none of them seemed to mind any of this, and now Caroline did not have to plan an escape from the room, merely leave without causing a disturbance.

The children had asked her if they all might put on a play for their parents before the party ended, and she was inclined to encourage it, but she had no notion of what was proper here. The older children were to ask their parents, and then they would see. Lord and Lady Mayfield seemed a good sort of people and seemed inclined to entertainment. The children had been invited to the party, after all, so why should they not have an evening together with the adults?

Oh, Miss Sheffield would have a great many opinions on the subject, and the thought of her aghast expression alone made Caroline wish to continue it.

"Miss Perkins!"

Caroline raised her head and saw one of the youngest children, little Sophie Mortimer, aged three, peeking her head out of the library. "Good evening, Sophie."

The dark-haired girl gestured for her to come. "We're all gathered, Miss Perkins. Come and read to us, won't you?"

"Of course, dear," Caroline replied with a smile, the tension in her chest beginning to unravel a little. "I'll come directly."

Sophie nodded her head and darted within the library.

Caroline let her smile fade and sagged against the wall for a moment.

Will had been so handsome tonight, as he was every night, but now that her heart was his, he grew more handsome and more dear with every moment. She would not be able to bear this for much longer. She would have to either confess herself or give up her situation.

She could not properly see a way to do either.

There was nothing proper about a tradesman's daughter being in love with the son of an earl, even if he would not inherit the title. There was nothing proper about forfeiting the companionship of Lady Ashby when she had been so very generous with her.

How proper was Caroline Perkins, tradesman's daughter and graduate of Miss Bell's?

Time alone would tell.

Caroline dipped her chin in a firm nod to herself, then straightened up, squared her shoulders, and strode to the library to read to the children, who did not care if she was rich or poor, proper or wild, pretty or plain.

Everything was far less complicated with them.

And less complicated was what she needed.

IF THERE WAS EVER a scene destined to make Will convinced that Caroline Perkins was the perfect woman, it would be this one before him now.

She had slipped out of the parlor not long ago, as she had taken to doing every evening, and this time he was determined to follow her. He wasn't sure where she went every night, but he had to know. They had almost no time together since coming to Parkway Manor unless they were dancing, and he craved any interaction with her at all.

He could not have imagined finding this.

She sat in the library with all of the children in the house around her, the two youngest girls in her lap. She had been reading the story of Cinderella and the glass slipper, and Will had arrived just after the beginning, so he'd managed to experience most of the story along with them. The little girls were enchanted by everything, while the boys had only wished to know when the fighting would begin, though the animals being turned to footmen and horses had delighted them. The littlest girls, Sophie and Lady Adele, snuggled close to Caroline, seeming far too comfortable and fortunate there.

Will knew it was fanciful, but with one of the girls bearing dark hair like his and the other being fair-haired like Caroline, it was all too easy to imagine them as their own daughters. To see them in the lap of their mother, enjoying a story read in dulcet tones, the voices of each character having distinct differences and sometimes comical airs. Caroline was a natural storyteller, and the warmest creature in the world. Any children of hers would adore her for eternity.

He could only hope he would be the one to give them to her, for he would adore her along with them.

When the happily ever after was attained, and the children clapped, Will slowly clapped himself. Caroline looked up and saw him as he was, leaning in the doorway to the library, his eyes trained on her. He smiled at her, warmth rising within up, and, he hoped, spreading into her.

Sophie patted her face to get her attention and begged for another story, but it was already far too late, so Caroline kissed her brow and promised two stories on the morrow, which seemed to satisfy her. Lady Adele refused to leave with the nursemaids who had come until Caroline hugged her a second time.

Will could easily understand that. He wondered if he could claim the same.

The other children were content with clasp of hands or touching their cheek, but all required something from Caroline. Had this happened every night? What fortunate children, and what a heart the woman he loved possessed. He watched as she gave personal attention to every child, her eyes darting to him with an increasing frequency, her complexion growing more flushed as she did so.

Will did not mind having to pause for the children before being alone with her. He would wait for an eternity with a smile and open arms.

Only when the room was empty save for the two of them did Caroline look back up at him, and he had not moved from his position. It occurred to him that, for all his being a perfect gentleman, he was positioned rather like a rake or rogue. Which version of him would she have preferred, he wondered.

He said nothing as he stared at her, could not. The face of perfection needed no words.

Caroline rose and slid a loose strand of hair behind her ear, turning to replace the book on the shelf.

"Do you have any idea, Caroline, what a remarkable woman you are?" he said, his voice low.

Caroline did not face him, though she stilled at the shelf. "I am nothing of the sort," she whispered, gripping the shelf slightly.

The wavering tone of her voice made him chuckle, and he shook his head. "How in the world do you not see it? How can you be so entirely unaware of yourself?"

Caroline swallowed hard and turned to face him, keeping her back against the bookcase. Her eyes were dark and luminous in the faint light of the room, and he moved towards her, watching her closely.

"I am aware of myself, sir," she murmured, her voice weak. "Utterly and completely aware, and that awareness only increases the more time I spend among people with whom I cannot belong."

Will's brow furrowed and he stepped closer. "It should," he said with a slow nod, his voice turning stern. "It should increase with such interaction. It is, after all, only natural."

Caroline closed her eyes, though Will had caught the sheen of tears before they had closed. Pain was etched across her glorious features, and he could not bear it.

He reached out and placed his fingers on her face, turning it up and smoothing away stray tears. "The more time you spend among us," he whispered, "we weak and simple creatures with whom you cannot belong, you ought to be more and more aware of the limitless ways you transcend all of us. We do not belong with you, Caroline, but we would each give our souls to try, could we see it."

Her eyes fluttered open, searching his with an eagerness that undid him.

He smiled very softly and stroked her cheek with the same sort of touch. "Will you never see yourself in truth?" he murmured as his fingers trailed from her cheek to her jaw.

"There is nothing to see," she breathed, trembling beneath his fingers. "I am the most ordinary sort of girl."

He cupped her face in both hands, his hold tightening just a little. "Would that I could rid such a thought from your head," he said gently, his energy and fervency for her rising. "There is nothing ordinary about you, Caroline Perkins, and everyone sees that but you. I am not a flatterer; I cannot tell you what it is that you are with flowery words and sonnets... But the barest, simplest truth I can give you is this: You are beyond words. And anyone who says less should be damned for such lies."

She inhaled the slightest gasp at that, which drew his attention to her lips.

Such perfect, full lips, and what a precious voice and soul proceeded from them.

Will dipped his head just as she rose up, and their lips melded together on a shared breath. They kissed over and over again, slowly, gently, tenderly, and without hesitation on either part.

Heaven could have no sweeter bliss than this.

Caroline was innocently eager, her lips moving against his, with his, as though part of the symphony of his heart. The music that only she could create for him. He cradled her face as though it were porcelain, keeping his attentions gentle and sweet, determined to make this moment sheer perfection for her.

But he could not overwhelm her, as he was being overwhelmed, and he began to gently pull back.

To his surprise, Caroline pressed closer against him and raised up for more, and he blindly complied. He took the kiss deeper, and she did the same, her hands sliding up to his neck and gripping with a tension that shook his knees. Will wrapped an arm around her as the other hand pressed her jaw closer to his. He moved them both, pressing them against the bookcase for some semblance of stability as she thoroughly unmanned him from the inside out. She fused herself to him, and he was only too willing to let her do so, to give himself over, heart, soul, and mouth.

He burned in every part of his body, heat and fire racing through his veins, and there was nothing to compare to it. His breath ached in his lungs, and he felt raw, open, and exposed in the arms of this woman.

He would gladly remain so.

Eventually, they drew apart, lingering but letting each other go, and Caroline sank weakly against the bookcase, his arm still locked around her. Will rested his head just over her shoulder against the nearest shelf, and then turned his face to kiss her cheek in a whisper of a kiss.

"You are everything, Caroline," he whispered against her skin. "Everything and so much more."

She shivered and curled into him more, and Will wondered if he would ever float back down to earth. He found himself praying to God that he might stay a while as thus.

Slowly, realizing he could not, he pulled away completely, and it was then that one of the maids came.

"Begging your pardon, Miss Perkins, but you are needed by Lady Ashby," the maid said with a bob.

She had no expression of surprise or dismay on her face, so the pair of them must have appeared as they always did.

In Will's mind, Caroline had never looked lovelier. He hadn't managed to dishevel her hair much, though her color was high and her lips bright. It was the most perfect temptation to kiss her again, but he refrained.

Caroline nodded, and hastened out of the library, avoiding his heated gaze and more heated body.

Will remained in his place, breathing slowly in and out, and only when he found control once more did he venture back out to the company.

As if heaven specifically wished to torment him, he found Caroline at the pianoforte playing for the company.

She was lost in her music, and Will was lost in her. From the graceful turn of her neck to the impressive motion of her fingers against the keys, he was in awe of her. Music was the perfect extension of all that she was, and he vowed there and then that, should she deign to wed him, he would beg her to fill their home with music. Both what she could play, and what they could create together.

For truly, she was the musician and he the instrument beneath her skilled fingers.

When she finished, the applause was extensive, as it ought to have been. Will went to her to help her from the pianoforte like the polite gentleman he was. Her dark eyes hit his as their hands touched, and it was as though they were back in the library once more. He could scarcely breathe, and he could see that she did not.

Love beyond expression surely shone through her eyes, and she would know it. But he could not look anywhere else, for he longed to have her back in his arms once more.

And surely, she knew that, too.

"I am terribly sorry, all, but I must retire," Lady Ashby proclaimed loudly. "Miss Perkins, dear, if you would...?"

Caroline's hand slipped from his, and Will felt the coldness of loss keenly. "Of course, my lady," Caroline said with her natural warmth, taking Lady Ashby's arm.

Lady Ashby looked at Caroline, then at Will, and smiled very slyly. "So sorry, Mr. Debenham. I appreciate your pain most keenly."

With a wink, she shuffled out with her now-flushed cheeked companion, whose dark eyes flicked to Will's knowingly.

Will grinned after them, both, thinking Lady Ashby might have been the finest woman of his acquaintance.

"I should probably see to my aunt," Sheffield murmured with some awkwardness as he made his own way out. "And Miss Perkins must have her due praise."

Despite everything, Sheffield's attention did not bother Will in the slightest. Caroline was *his* heart's desire, and he was sure now that she felt just as much for him. No matter what Sheffield wanted or thought, Will no longer saw him as a rival. He could not love Caroline as Will did, and there was no risk of her being swept away by any other.

She was his, and his alone.

Tomorrow Will would ask for her hand, and after what had passed between them this evening, he had every reason to hope that her answer would be a favorable one.

CHAPTER 11

The docks were quiet in the mornings.

That seemed a significant thing for Caroline to forget yet forget it she had. It was only recently that she had experienced it once more.

Only five days, to be precise.

Five days since her world collapsed on itself, and everything changed.

Caroline sat at the window of Mrs. Briggs' boarding house kitchen, ignoring the bustle of the place while they prepared breakfast for the guests staying there. She was not one of the staff as yet, only a quiet boarder with the freedom to move as she wished, by orders of Mrs. Briggs herself. And this quiet corner of the kitchen, out of the way and unobserved by most, was where she chose more often than not.

Only five days ago, perhaps six, if one counted travel, the letter had come to Caroline while at Parkway Manor. It had come by express, of all things, though thankfully it had not disturbed any of the household. Most of the guests and the family had still been entertaining themselves in the parlor with their usual evening activities.

Caroline and Lady Ashby had only just retired, though Caroline had considered it to be a lucky escape from the delicious and heady attentions of Will Debenham.

Oh, how he had kissed her that night! And how she had kissed him! She had never known such freedom and exhilaration as she had found in his arm in the library. Such dreams had swirled in her mind in the aftermath, even while she had played the pianoforte for the gathering. Things she had never dared to hope for herself were suddenly possible, and joy beyond imagination at the tips of her fingers.

Then the letter had come, just as she had settled Lady Ashby into her bed.

The letter was from Mr. Coolidge, her father's man of business, and it appeared that Caroline's father had indeed found a way to ruin her. Mr. Coolidge had not gone into much detail then, but Caroline had since learned that her father had managed to convince the necessary parties that his daughter was, in fact, not his daughter. She was, he claimed, the illegitimate daughter of his late brother, and thus no longer entitled to the earnings set up for her.

In short, Mr. Coolidge lamented, Caroline's fortune was gone. All of it.

All she had to her name was the pin money she had received from Lady Ashby, which was a pittance, considering her greater kindness was to sponsor her in Society. She would have nothing to live on but those meager earnings, and, perhaps worst of all, it was even more impossible for her to have Will.

Mr. Debenham, she reminded herself. The distance between them was greater than ever, and utterly impassable.

She was ruined.

Caroline had confided in Lady Ashby at once, quietly relating everything she had not dared to express before, and, much to her credit, none of it seemed to perturb her ladyship in the slightest.

"My dear Caroline, how hard this must be for you," she had murmured, putting a hand to Caroline's cheek. "There will be nothing I can do for you at first. The ramifications of such revelations will be catastrophic, you know."

Caroline could only nod to that, unable to meet her ladyship's gaze.

But Lady Ashby had tipped her chin up and given her a severe look. "But after the first of it, and the worst of it, you may be quite sure I shall be able to do quite a good deal. Let us leave first thing in the morning, and when we return to London, I will lay it all out for you. Take heart, Caroline. At last, I may have something to truly offer you." She had smiled and insisted they both get a wink or two of sleep, leaving Caroline to silently sputter to herself.

It was an impossible idea, Lady Ashby doing anything for her in her present situation, but she had also learned never to doubt the woman. There had been no course but to do as it was suggested and attempt to sleep.

They had left Parkway Manor as quietly as possible the next morning, only informing the necessary parties of the Mayfields and Mr. Sheffield. Lady Ashby and Mr. Sheffield saw Caroline back to London, claiming to their hosts that her ladyship was too weary to continue the party. They did not make any farewells to the others, so as to not raise questions or suspicions. Mr. Sheffield had assured Caroline that he would help her, but she did not, and would not, expect that, nor deserve it.

Upon returning to London, Caroline took her leave of Lady Ashby and of Ashby House almost from the moment of her arrival. Tearfully, Lady Ashby declared she would hire Caroline in earnest when she retired to the country after Christmas. It seemed that, for all their time together, her ladyship despaired of being worth anything to Caroline beyond opportunity, and she was only too pleased to, eventually, be able to keep her.

More than that, she vowed she would still help Caroline to find a respectable husband. It was a kind thought, but Caroline had little hope of its coming to pass.

Mr. Sheffield, who had become friend and almost brother as well as protector, insisted on seeing Caroline daily, despite the poor nature of her current situation on Fleet Street. Mrs. Briggs had given her lodging until matters were more settled in her life, as Caroline could not remain with Lady Ashby. Her niece would still be in residence after the house party, and Miss Sheffield would want nothing to do with her at all. Lady Ashby would not see Caroline further abused, for which Caroline was most grateful.

"Caro, angel," Mrs. Briggs called from the stairs to the main of the boarding house. "Mr. Sheffield is here."

Caroline sighed and slid down from her perch. "He is early today."

"Yes, lamb, but he is such a dear heart." Mrs. Briggs smiled with a motherly warmth. "I shall bring you both some scones by and by."

"Thank you," Caroline said, squeezing her hands as she left.

Mrs. Briggs always allowed them use of her private parlor, away from the listening ears and curious eyes of the other guests, and, now that Caroline was no fine lady, no one saw the need for any kind of chaperone.

"David," Caroline greeted with a smile as she saw Mr. Sheffield there, now insisting on informality between them.

He rose and smiled, looking her up and down quickly. "You look improved this morning, Caroline. Fewer shadows and your smile not so stretched."

She had grown used to his directness over the last few days and found it quite refreshing. She nodded and gestured for him to sit. "I slept well. I haven't quite decided what to do as yet, but my father has not tried to reach me, so I have time."

David shook his head firmly. "I wish you would let me prosecute him, Caroline. I know a great many men who could arrange quite the case against him."

Caroline sighed. "It would serve no purpose. He has claimed I am illegitimate, and there is nothing to refute it. Of course, there is nothing to say that I am, and the mystery of my birth will, in truth, remain just that. He has set about to restore the business, and all seems to be going well there. Mr. Coolidge hopes he can salvage something for me, as Uncle Paul was very careful with his will and his finances, but I cannot hope for much. Still, he has set up a trust for me with some portion of the profits in the restored company, and my father knows nothing of it. I am grateful for his thoughtfulness, though the earnings he can set aside will be meager indeed."

They had been over this time and again, and David's expression was always laced with the same amount of disgruntlement.

"We received some calling cards for you, you know," he murmured, sitting forward and resting his arms on his knees. "Miss Foster, a Miss Elliot, and a Miss Grey. Friends of yours?"

Tears rushed into Caroline's eyes, and she nodded hastily. "The best of them, yes."

He reached into his coat and pulled the cards out, handing them to her. "I take it you have not written to them."

Now she shook her head. "No. How can I? There is nothing to be done, and I cannot have anyone racing needlessly off to my rescue."

"You are not less of a person for asking for help, Caroline," David insisted earnestly. "Some of us truly care and will do all we can for you."

"I know," she murmured, smiling at him. "If I thought it would help, believe me, I would let anyone. I have no pride left to uphold."

And it was true. She had never been lower than she was at the present. She would have actual employment after Christmas, and until then, she would be as much use to Mrs. Briggs as possible. She may write to her friends eventually, once she had settled, but not now.

Not yet.

David sat back in his chair, exhaling in irritation. "Well, Anna returned to Ashby House, for whatever that's worth. She is a vain, puffed up girl with venom in her veins, and she proved that all too well. Still, only a few more weeks in Ashby House with her, and she'll be off somewhere again. And when my sister is returned to our family, having made no lasting friends nor matches, and failing to secure my aunt's willingness to sponsor her again, Lady Ashby will welcome you back with open arms, and a proper salary."

"She is very kind," Caroline murmured, smiling fondly. "Please assure her that I will accept, and that I miss her so terribly."

Now David smiled at her. "I will. She misses you as well and bemoans your loss on a regular basis. It makes Anna furious. I love it."

Caroline bit back a laugh, covering her mouth.

David shook his head. "So, you can laugh after all. I wondered if you did."

"Yes, I can laugh," Caroline replied softly, her mind turning to Mr. Debenham in a moment. "I am only particular as to when I do. And with whom."

There was a lingering moment of silence, and David's expression told Caroline he knew only too well where her thoughts lay.

But he said nothing about it, and neither did she.

"Will you keep a secret if I tell you?" he asked suddenly, his smile growing.

Caroline looked at him in surprise. "Of course, I will."

He nodded once. "I have given my heart away, Caroline. Entirely and without reservation. And you will appreciate this for what it is worth and what it means, but she is the daughter of a sea captain from Bristol."

Caroline gaped at him, torn between delight and horror. "David…"

David grinned at her sheepishly. "A poor girl with no dowry at all, but the sweetest temperament I have ever found. I met her by pure chance while I was there before the season, and I cannot get her out of my head. We have been writing to each other constantly since we have been parted as part of our courtship, and I am convinced that she is my better half. I fear ever being able to bring her into my family, knowing the nature of positions and stations as I do. What if she should never be accepted despite her wonderful nature?"

"All very valid thoughts," Caroline said, more to herself than to anyone else.

"You have settled many of those fears, you know."

She reared back. "Pardon?"

He nodded fervently. "You have given me hope, in your situation. My sister may never fully accept it, but that is her loss, not mine. And after seeing my aunt with you, I confessed the whole thing to Lady Ashby just last night. She has led me to believe that she would not be averse to meeting her. I cannot tell you how much that has encouraged for the future with Bess and myself."

Caroline could not help but to smile at him, even if that smile did not linger. "I am relieved if I am proof that stations mean less than nature," she told him with all the warmth in the world. "But I must remind you that the world is not nearly so kind nor understanding as your aunt, nor Mr. Debenham. Anyone who had seen me in any of the ballrooms this Season would attest to that."

David smiled and said, "Deb told me people would think me unconventional and unprincipled to do such a thing. And then he said 'To hell with convention and principle, Sheffield. Marry her, and damn the rest of them'." He shrugged with a grin. "I am inclined to agree, and now have the strength to do so, if she will have such a coward as I."

There was nothing cowardly at all in David Sheffield, but Caroline smiled all the same. "Well, if she should find any difficulty in doing so, send her to me. I shall set her to rights soon enough."

He seemed surprised. "You would speak for me?" he asked, tilting his head curiously. "And support such a difference in station and situation?"

Caroline found herself surprised by his surprise. "Of course."

"And yet you rebuffed Deb."

A painful wince flashed across Caroline's face, bringing a matching slash of agony across her chest. She looked away with a rough swallow. "It was right."

"No, I think not," he persisted, leaning forward to take her hand. "Caroline, if I can have my Bess, why can you not have Deb?"

"It is not that simple," she informed him, feeling her heart crack. "Bess only lacks fortune, but her father is respectable. My former fortune was from trade. My father is a drunk merchant who gambles, whores, and steals fortunes. I was illiterate until I was twelve, and my language and accent are so coarse I would be barred from any parlor in my natural state. Miss Bell's school only taught me how to hide the truth of myself. It not a mere step of station. It is a flying leap of inhuman dimension."

"He doesn't see it that way," David murmured, squeezing her hands, "and nor do I."

"Your blindness is not my misfortune," Caroline whispered, "but yours."

David shook his head and released her hands. "I will not let you speak further on this topic. We are sure to disagree. Tell me how you are getting on here."

Caroline was grateful for the change in topic. She dared not tell him the truth of her heart, that she ached for Will, that her nights were filled with tears for the pain, that she ought to have tried when she at least had a fortune of respectability. Now to have nothing, not even hope, was crushing in its devastation.

She only shrugged. "I am well and whole, and I am working hard to earn my board with Mrs. Briggs, though she is loath to let me. 'Ye be a fine lady now, Caro, and 'tain't right to work 'ee so.' "

David chuckled at the impression. "Spot on, very good."

"She is such a dear," Caroline said with a sigh, "but I am no fine lady, and I never shall be. I only ever pretended at one."

"Not so, my dear," David scolded gently. "Not so."

But it was so. It always had been, now more than ever. Her future was not so bleak as it might have once been. She would be a companion to Lady Ashby in truth soon, and that was a very respectable position for a girl. She may even yet hope for that quiet country curate.

If her heart could let go.

PACING WAS NOT A GENTLEMANLY HABIT. Will had been told this all his life.

He had never managed to rid himself of the habit, so it seemed that he was not, after all, a perfect gentleman.

He could not have cared less about that at this moment. He'd give up absolutely everything he had ever wanted before he'd met Caroline Perkins just to have her.

It had taken him long enough to put the pieces together of what had happened and finally take charge of what he wanted in life. Now he was pacing as he waited for the last and most crucial piece of the puzzle to come down.

He'd taken great care not to leave his name when he had come, not sure how she would respond to his visit.

Her reaction would tell him everything he needed to know. After her vanishing in the early morning hours at Parkway Manor, taking his heart with her, Will had doubted everything he had ever felt or thought. He had blamed himself for frightening her off after their liaison in the library, for pressing his suit with too much vigor, for anything and everything he thought could possibly have caused her flight.

Will had avoided Sheffield and everything to do with Caroline for days, and then he'd shook himself from the fog of his stupidity, determined to discover the truth and recover something, if he could.

Now, at last, he was here.

Here was where she had fled, back to where her story had begun. Where she saw herself as ever belonging, despite all that she had accomplished and become. He could almost see the attraction, given the hum of activity and the relative anonymity of the place.

But not for Caroline.

Not for them.

Mrs. Briggs, lovely and warm woman that he took her to be, had scurried away not long ago to fetch Caroline, and he wondered if she were spending the time gossiping up there while he was fair perishing down here.

But then he heard footsteps, and he turned to face the door, clasping his hands behind him in an attempt to look calm.

In truth, he was anything but.

Caroline entered the parlor and froze, her eyes latching onto him, her breath faltering. She was more radiant than he remembered, if a little gaunt for his taste, looking as lovely and perfect as she ever did. Her hair was plaited simply, saving the smallest crown encircling her head, and her gown was plain and threadbare. Still, to him, she was ever the goddess of his heart.

He couldn't say a word; everything was beyond expression.

He nearly smiled when Caroline swallowed, and her legs shifted beneath her skirts as though she would flee the room. "I would chase you," he murmured, answering the action she could have been contemplating.

The widening of her eyes told him his impression had been correct.

Still Caroline stared, and something in her expression softened and turned tender, her fingers slowly curling and uncurling at her sides. He prayed that could only mean she wanted to fly at him. Wanted him to sweep her up. Wanted his arms around her.

Taking a chance, he smiled slightly. "I would oblige you."

She released a rough exhale by way of answer, and Will knew then that he was lost. He knew her as intimately as he knew himself, and there would be no other for him ever.

Her lips formed the beginning of a question, her eyes beginning to swim, but no sound emerged from her.

"Why am I here?" he asked, taking pity on her and vocalizing the question she did not ask.

Caroline nodded shakily.

Will shook his head slowly. "My darling Caroline is it not clear enough?" he said in a low, almost rumbling voice he felt it in his chest. "I will only be where you are. There is nothing I want more than to be with you."

"You can't," she replied, her voice trembling as a stray tear fell from her eyes.

He stepped towards her with care. "You will not let me? You do not want me? Or you think I cannot feel as I do?"

"I... I..." She could not find the words, it seemed, even as her eyes remained on his, unmoving and barely blinking.

He smiled, loving her for all the ignorance of her own majesty. "Do you know what hurts me the most?"

She did not answer, though her breathing became fairly erratic as he approached.

"You are content to torment me for eternity because you think so low of yourself." He shook his head slowly, the pain of the last few weeks resurfacing. "When you left Parkway Manor, without a word, without seeing me, without... I thought you were fleeing *me*, Caroline. I thought I had gone too far, presumed too much, that you could never care for me as I did for you."

"No," Caroline breathed, the word catching on a hiccup that made his pulse jump with hope.

Will wet his lips, his own emotions rising. "But I knew what I felt," he continued, his voice lower and a bit strained. "I knew how you had captivated me from the first, how all this time I have struggled against it, not for your station or your past or anything you might think, but because it seemed so impossible to hope." He continued slowly towards her, giving her every opportunity to flee if she chose. "I have loved you, my sweet Caroline, for so long, and yet so very brief. I have loved you when you were rich, I have loved you when you were poor, I have loved you when you had little accomplishment, I have loved you when you took London by storm..."

Caroline released a soft scoffing sound, then covered her mouth, and he smiled very briefly at the sign of humor in her.

"I have loved you when you were sad," he murmured, coming ever closer, "and when you were so filled with joy it stole my breath. I have loved you, my love, as every man dares to imagine he can. You, who are so blind to the truth of who you are, who will ever need reminding of your worth, who will ever rise above all limitations... It is you and you alone. It was always and will always be you for me."

He stopped before her, the distance enough that they did not touch, but it could be easily remedied.

"I want nothing more than to have you, Caroline," he said, his eyes tracing her features as if his fingers did so, "as my wife, my lover, the mother of my children, the dream of my nights, the joy of my days... I will have you in any way that I can. You or no one. I will ask you every day for the rest of our lives because I love you too much to bear a single day without you knowing it. So, if you can find a place in that warm and generous heart of yours for me, will you have me as well?"

Caroline shook from head to toe at this point, and tears coursed down her cheeks unchecked. She opened her mouth to speak, but all that came was one broken gasp of a sob.

Will reached out to brush her tears away, her skin like the warmth of the sun. "Oh, my darling." He cupped her face in his hands, stepping closer and gazing deeply into her eyes. "Caroline, I beg you... Say yes."

She immediately crumpled in his hold and buried her face against him. "Yes," she cried, the word muffled against his coat. "Oh, yes." She shuddered in his hold, clinging to him desperately.

Exhaling a slow sigh of relief, Will wrapped his arms around her and pulled her close, letting her cry. He tilted her head back and ran his lips tenderly over her face, tracing the path of every tear, then settling his mouth on her own.

She responded at once, leaving him in no doubt that the last few days and weeks had been just as much of an agony for her. She matched him in yearning and seemed to be reaching for something within him. It was the very same thing he sought in her, and they had a lifetime to find it. To keep finding it. To treasure it.

Her legs soon gave out, and he swept her up in his arms, carrying her to Mrs. Briggs' settee, and settling there with her. He stroked her hair and kissed her gently, over and over again, grazing and brushing kisses that spoke of everything that had passed and everything that would come.

Caroline broke off suddenly, crying anew.

"What is it, love?" he asked her tenderly, stroking her jaw. "What makes you cry so?"

"I love you," she whispered, shaking her head and running her fingers along his cheek. "I love you so much."

Will felt as if the sun had come out for the first time in his entire life and smiled at her. "And that makes you cry?"

She nodded, wrapping her arms around his neck and pulling him close. "I can't help it. I'm sorry."

He looked heavenward as she clung to him, then gently pulled her head away from his body and held her fast. "Never apologize for loving me." His voice caught on the words. "Never. Nor for your tears. I will kiss away each and every one and hold you while you cry. You don't have to be strong and serene and composed, Caroline. Not with me. Never with me."

"You might find me a watering pot, then," she muttered, swiping at her cheeks and nose.

He grinned. "I hope so. I can be very good at comforting you, and I look forward to it. Cry all you want, I'm ready to serve."

Surprising them both, Caroline tossed her head back and laughed, her throat dancing with the sound, and it filled Will's soul.

He laughed with her, then captured her face again and looked at her with love and adoration as she beamed at him. "You laughed," he breathed, smiling tenderly. "It is the most beautiful sound in the world, just as I knew it would be. I've changed my mind, love. Don't cry. Laugh. Laugh every day. But only for me."

Caroline slid her hands around his neck, her fingers lacing into his hair. She nodded and pulled him close, touching her brow to his. "Only for you, my love. Despite what anybody has ever said, I have only ever truly felt beautiful with you."

Such a simple, sweet, impossible statement, and it touched him to his core. He kissed her softly. "I see you for who and what you are, Caroline. And I love you even more with every passing day. When we're old and grey, my love, there will be nothing left of me but love of you."

She smiled, and laughed very softly, brushing her nose along his. "I see you as well, Will. And it's more than I dared hope for."

Will grinned and pulled back to give her the sort of look he imagined those rogues and cads gave when they were charming a pretty miss. "Call me Will again. It makes me wild to kiss you."

Caroline returned his grin, and cupped his face, her dark eyes searing his. "Will, would you please kiss me again?"

"Of course, Miss Perkins," he murmured as her lips descended upon hers again. "Always."

EPILOGUE

"So, we are to spend Christmas with his family in York. Lord and Lady Sedley will arrive tomorrow to meet me, and Will's brother, the heir to the earldom, came to London only yesterday. Mr. Sheffield is to walk me down the aisle when we do wed, his sister will send her regrets, we know, and Lady Ashby is to furnish my trousseau, despite my objections."

"Oh, Caroline!" Adelaide sniffled, her hands flying to her cheeks. "It's so perfect! Could you ever imagine anything so perfect?"

"Of course, she didn't," Jo scoffed, waving a hand. "None of us really imagined the sort of sweeping romance Caroline has had." She looked at Caroline speculatively. "How did Lady Ashby take the news?"

Caroline blushed and shrugged. "She approves most heartily and cried in earnest when Will asked her for my hand, although she is most distressed that I will not be available to be her companion now."

Penelope shook her head, smiling reluctantly. "She will get over that I am sure. Though I am not sure I will forgive you for some time for not telling us about your father."

The others nodded, though there was warmth and kindness in their features.

"I know," Caroline murmured in apology. "I just... I wasn't sure what to do, and I couldn't bear to impose... Will says it is due to a faulty lack of vision, both of myself and of those who care for me."

"I can agree with that," Penelope said with firmness. "I've always said that there is nothing wrong with trade."

Johanna rolled her eyes. "Penelope, there is some difference between your situation and Caroline's, even you can see that."

"Of course, I can," Penelope shot back. "But there is nothing wrong with it."

Adelaide shook her head and took Caroline's hand. "Ignore them. We are all so happy for you. And we adore your Mr. Debenham, too!"

Caroline blushed further as she looked across the room at her handsome intended, who was watching her with a knowing smile. "Oh, Addy, he loves me so, and I cannot breathe for the sensation. We will never be conventional, but then, I never was, and he loves me just as I am. And I love him as he is."

"And really," Johanna murmured, sounding far away, "who could wish for more?"

Caroline looked at the others, then they all looked at Johanna. "Everything all right?"

Johanna shook her head and beamed brightly. "Of course! Just romanticizing. Have you settled on where you will live?"

"Will has a few estates for us to see in Derbyshire," Caroline admitted, looking back at him with all the love in the world. "But no matter where we live, Will has asked Mrs. Briggs to be our housekeeper. Can you imagine?" She laughed and shook her head. "She shut up the boarding house straightaway and is already on her way into the country! We don't even have an estate, but she has gone. We shall have her pies the rest of our days, and Will is very much looking forward to the prospect."

The girls all laughed, and Caroline laughed with them, though the joy in her heart spanned across the room to the man laughing there for no reason except that she was. Her joy was his joy, and his light her light.

Surely there was nothing more beautiful in the world than a love like this.

What fortunate creatures were they.

PREVIEW OF THE SPINSTER

*B*undled up in her warmest coat, Jo touched her forehead to the chilled window of the carriage that was to take her home.

Home to Holten Park.

Her family's country estate.

The place of a happy childhood.

As well as the greatest tragedy of Jo's young life.

Snow swirled through the air and lay in heaps and mounds all around her as the carriage fought its way onward. Heaving a deep sigh, Jo glanced at the dim outlines of a world that had once been as familiar to her as the back of her hand. Countless days, her feet had carried her through the tall-stemmed grass in summer and across the iced-over lake in winter. She had climbed trees and found her way through thorny bushes. On rare occasions, she had even dared to swim in the lake, enjoying the cooling water against her heated skin.

Wild, her grandmother had called her, an amused twinkle in the old lady's eyes.

Johanna's mother had preferred the term *unruly,* her straight nose rising in haughty displeasure whenever she'd caught her daughter in a less than lady-like situation.

Still, to this day, Lady Rawdon was not aware of even half of the unsuitable activities Johanna had undertaken whenever she had climbed out of her window and run off to find another adventure. Jo much preferred it this way.

Four years had passed since the day of *the tragedy.*

Four years that Jo had spent away from home and at school where she was to learn *suitable behaviour fit for a young lady* as her mother had phrased it. *The tragedy* had been the final straw, and so Lady Rawdon had sent her fourteen-year-old daughter to Miss Bell's Finishing School for Young Ladies, hoping and praying that for once Johanna would do as she was told.

Four years had passed since then, and Johanna had done her utmost to please her mother and become the accomplished, young woman Lady Rawdon had always wanted her to be. After all, if she had been that young woman from the first, Owen would still be alive today.

Out of the corner of her eye, Jo caught sight of Holten Park, a stately manor with the old charm of an ancient castle. Snow covered its roof and lay draped over the grounds like a blanket. Ice crystals grew at the edges of the many windows allowing in the sparkling light of a sunny winter's day. It was a peaceful sight, always had been, and yet, Jo could not keep a painful knot from forming in her belly.

Glancing across the seat at the rotund and currently-snoring woman Lady Rawdon had sent to escort her daughter from Bath back to Holten Park, Jo smiled, feeling a renewed sense of adventure stir in her blood.

In the past four years, she had barely felt it. Perhaps it was this place that reminded her of the young girl she had once been. The young girl she had buried with Owen.

The young girl that seemed to have survived somewhere deep inside her.

The moment the carriage pulled to a halt outside the snow-covered front steps, Jo pulled her coat tighter around her shoulders and then opened the door before the footman had any chance of approaching. Feeling the cold winter's air touch her cheeks, she breathed in deeply and then hopped to the ground in a very unlady-like fashion, her booted feet sinking into the snow.

Excitement bubbled up in her blood, and a familiar smile claimed her features.

"Miss–"

Spinning around to face Mr. Carter, the coachman, Jo put a finger to her lips, bidding him to remain silent.

All but rolling his eyes, Mr. Carter looked at her, the faint traces of a smile coming to his face as he sighed. His hair had gone grey since she had last seen him, but his blue eyes still twinkled with the same understanding Jo had often seen there before.

After giving him a quick smile, Jo dashed away, rounding the house from the west, her feet carrying her through the deep snow. With each step, her limbs grew heavier and wetness seeped through the skirts. Still, Jo's cheeks shone with eagerness, and she could not remember having felt this alive in the past four years.

Craning her head, Jo looked over her shoulder before she stepped onto the terrace, carefully picking her way across the frozen ground to the double-winged doors. Her heart beat fast in her chest, and old memories stirred, urging her on. Her fingers reached out to touch the silver handle, and she held her breath as her hand closed around it, pushing it downward.

With a silent creak, the door slid open and a welcoming warmth washed over Johanna's chilled skin. Quickly, she cast a look around the empty drawing room, then stepped inside, her heart delighting in the small puddles her feet left behind on the hardwood floor.

Jo knew that her mother would be in fits once she found out that her daughter had sneaked into the house like a common thief instead of entering through the front door and greeting her parents as any good daughter would. Still, in that moment, Jo could not deny the little girl she had kept silent for four long years.

Brushing her boots off on the Persian rug, Jo silently crossed the room and leaned her head against the door. When all remained quiet, she stepped out into the hall and did her best to move stealthily as she listened for sounds of someone approaching.

As though to welcome her home, no one crossed her path and Jo hastened up the stairs to her old bedchamber without a look back. Laughter tickled the back of her throat, and she clamped her lips shut, lest it spill forth and alert someone.

Only when the door was firmly closed behind her did Jo exhale the breath she had been holding, a large smile claiming her face as her eyes swept over the room that still looked as it always had, as though she had never been gone from Holten Park.

Her bed had been freshly made, sheets of lilac and violet warming the room, a stark contrast to the snow-covered treetops visible through the three large windows opening to the east. The wood was a dark mahogany, but thin and elegantly carved, giving the room a feminine touch. Two large shelves were filled with books about distant worlds and adventures that could be had for real if only one had not been born a woman.

To Lady Rawdon's dismay, her daughter much preferred the written word to more lady-like pastimes such as drawing and embroidery. During her stay at Miss Bell's, Jo had made an honest effort to master these qualities so highly regarded not only by her mother but society at large. Still, to this day, her fingers seemed to be possessed by a will of their own whenever she picked up a brush or a needle. Nothing good had ever resulted from these endeavours, and by now, Jo knew that nothing ever would.

"I thought I'd find you here, my dear."

AFTERWORD

Want to hear about future releases and upcoming events for Rebecca Connolly?

Sign up for the monthly Wit and Whimsy at: www.rebeccaconnolly.com

ABOUT THE AUTHOR

Rebecca Connolly writes romances, both period and contemporary, because she absolutely loves a good love story. She has been creating stories since childhood, and there are home videos to prove it! She started writing them down in elementary school and has never looked back. She currently lives in the Midwest, spends every spare moment away from her day job absorbed in her writing, and is a hot cocoa addict.

Also by Rebecca Connolly

The Arrangements:
    An Arrangement of Sorts
    Married to the Marquess
    Secrets of a Spinster
    The Dangers of Doing Good
    The Burdens of a Bachelor
    A Bride Worth Taking
    A Wager Worth Making
    A Gerrard Family Christmas

The Spinster Chronicles:
    The Merry Lives of Spinsters
    The Spinster and I
    Spinster and Spice

Coming Soon:
   My Fair Spinster

Made in United States
North Haven, CT
19 November 2023

44252758R00093